Evil never sleeps

Patricia Wood

Contents

Chapter 1

5 Years Ago

He could hear his father's drunken footsteps coming up the stairs. Heavy grunts and groans echoed in the air. If he took in a deep breath of air, he could probably smell the alcohol that was obviously on his father.

'Drunk-ass bastard.' he thought to himself.

His hand slowly reaches toward his bedside table. He grabs hold of the heel of a knife and hides it under the covers, keeping it in reach. Staring at the door, his eyes were adjusted to the dark and was prepared for anything.

Soon his door flew open and banged against the wall. He wasn't affected by the noise as he is used to it. His grip on the knife tightened as he prepares for the storm to come.

"Wake up you little bitch." his father slurred.

"Get away from me." the boy growled. He sits up straight but kept the knife hidden. "I'm warning you." he threatened.

His father only laughed drunkly as he took the threat as empty words. "What will you do about it?" he challenged. He reaches out to grab his son by the throat. But just before his farther's hand touched him, he was stabbed straight through the palm.

"I will simply kill you." the son responded gleefully.

A loud scream escaped his father as he wrenches his hand away. He stumbles backwards out of the room and falls on to his back. "You little bastard!" he screamed.

"I'm the bastard? Who was the one who tormented me, raped me, and beat me ever since Mom left us? Huh!?" his son challenged him. He jumps out of bed and walks tauntingly toward his father. "I've had enough of your shit! It's time for you to pay!" With a swift move, he sinks the knife in to his father's foot. The blade slipped through his foot, and the tip touches the floor from the other side.

His father screamed loudly as his foot bled. "STOP!" he begged.

"NO!" his son screamed.

Ripping the knife out of his foot, the son jumps on top of his overweight father and starts to stab him. He kept both hands on the knife to keep a grip from slipping. Blood started to splatter all over the floor, the walls, and on the son.

It felt as if all pain and stress he had felt for so many years just lifted off his shoulders. The more he stabbed the bastard, the more he became happy. He starts to stab faster. Letting out loud laughter as he did so. He felt as if he could do this forever.

Flashing blue and red lights stopped him. He stops his repeated stabs to take a breath. His father was long dead. The lifelessness in his father's eyes made him smile.

The wailing sound of sirens caught his attention. Looking out the window that stood at the end of the hall. He saw police cars standing outside the house. "Aw. I can't continue my fun." he said disappointed. He looks down at his father with a lopsided grin. "At least I got my revenge." he said gleefully.

Quickly, he jumps off the corpse and ran to the bedroom that stood opposite of his room. He snatches a backpack he had lying on the guest bed. Then he opens the window and climbs out. Just as he hears the front door break down from downstairs.

"NYPD!" screamed out a powerful voice.

'Too late, coppers. I'm already gone.' he thought as he jumps out the window.

Chapter 2

P resent Day

"Cody, wake up or you'll be late for school!" shouted a woman along with loud banging against his door.

Underneath a pillow, an eye opens to reveal a honey brown color. "I'm awake, Ms. Elias. I'll be down in a minute!" he shouted in a muffle.

Slowly sliding out of bed, he was startled awake when he steps on something that moved. Cody jumped about two feet in the air and looks at what he stepped on, now wide awake. Finding it was Ms. Elias's pet iguana Izzy.

"Really, Izzy? I thought I put you in your tank." Cody said to the giant reptile. The female reptile just stares at him with lazy eyes. "Ugh." he said with an eye roll. He bends down and picks up the reptile. The creature wasn't that heavy but she did squirm a lot when she didn't want to be held. This was one of those moments.

The large reptile squirmed and sank her claws into his skin. She wrapped her tail around his arm and tried to throw herself out of his arms. "Stop squirming! I'm trying to put you in your damn home!" Cody yelled as he practically stuffs the iguana in her tank. Only for Izzy to smack him with her tail, and she runs out of the room.

"Ms. Elias, Izzy's going down the stairs moody again!" Cody called out as he puts on a black t-shirt and changes into a pair of blue jeans.

"Thank you for the warning!" Ms. Elias called back.

Cody couldn't help but laugh at her response. He has known Ms. Elias for nearly a year and she is like a sister to him than a foster mother. For five years, Cody has been in the foster care system. His parents passed away in a home invasion. Cody was there when it happened, hiding in the basement and in a dark corner. That was where the police had found him.

His tarp-covered parents still haunted his dreams. Only twelve at the time, it was truly horrifying to see his parents dead.

Taking in a deep breath, Cody looks at himself through the mirror. He had long, shaggy brown hair, a strong jaw, and high cheekbones. His eyes were the same as his father's while he had his mother's hair. Cody wished he didn't look so much like his mother. It makes it harder to cope.

After changing clothes and packing his books in to his backpack, he leaves his room and heads downstairs. The hallway was small with three doors. One was to a bathroom, the other was to Ms. Elias's room, and the last was his bedroom. There was another bedroom and it was downstairs.

Cody reached the bottom step and had to jump over a cranky Izzy who slept on it. He could hear her snores that re-sembled growls. Valuing unbruised ankles, he silently walks to the kitchen.

He was greeted with the smell of scrambled eggs and bacon. A very casual meal in the household. He sits down in a table that was beside the kitchen counter. "No pancakes? Usually you go for the full bed and breakfast course." Cody joked. He grabs a green apple and takes a bite.

"We're out of the pancake mix. Either way, you need a good meal for school." said Ms. Elias. When Cody looked up at her, he felt his heart swell at the sight.

Ms. Elias wore a light purple, sleeveless dress that stopped at her knees. Her skin was a fair pale with freckles dazzling her cheeks. Short black hair reached the middle of her neck, revealing a butterfly tattoo in the center of back of her neck. Beautiful green eyes stared down at the scrambled eggs she was cooking. Despite being 30, she looked at least 25.

"You have work today, Ms. Elias?"

"How many times have I told you to call me Sarah! No more formalities!"

She tried to look threatening with the spatula but Cody just made a snort. "So work?" he asked again. Sarah calmed down immediately and says,"No work today. I have a day off."

A plate of scrambled eggs, bacon, and toast was laid down in front of Cody. "Now eat up. The bus will be here in ten minutes." Sarah said.

The smell was making Cody's mouth water, and he didn't stop himself from digging in. Sarah's food was undeniably delicious. She was the top chef at a famous restaurant for a reason. Even if it's the simplest of meals.

He scarfed down the food in under three minutes. "Fank ou!" Cody said with a mouthful of eggs. "Swallow!" Sarah said before tapping Cody's head with a wooden spoon.

After swallowing, Cody laughs. He picks up his plate and carries it to the sink. "Im going to search for jobs after school. So I may not be back for a few hours." Cody said as he washes his hands after placing his plate in the sink. "Be back before six, that's the rule." Sarah said.

"Got it!" Cody said as he grabs his backpack and heads out of the house. Avoiding a sleeping Izzy who changed to a different sleeping spot that laid in front of the door. "Are you sure you're not a cat?" he asked curiously. He steps over Izzy and quietly opens the front door and leaves.

The October air was chilly but still had some warmth in it. Goosebumps ran up his arm and he sighs happily. Cody enjoyed the cold air. He grew up in Minnesota so he could handle the snow better than others can. Unlike most, he didn't need a jacket because New York was nothing compared to Minnesota.

He walked down the sidewalk toward the bus stop. His walks always gave him time to think. Helped him think about how he was going to do once he turned eighteen in three months. Sarah said he could stay with her till he went to college and he could always stay with her. Cody didn't want to be a bother so he wanted to make it into the world as soon as he could.

The walk was quiet with the exception of tweeting birds. The wind pressed lightly against his skin and made his hair flutter. Strands of hair fell in front of his eyes but he didn't brush them away. Many times Sarah asked if he wanted to cut his hair, but he refuses, saying he wanted a reminder of his mother.

Cody didn't realize he was at the bus stop till he bumps into someone. He jumps a few feet in the air and looks at who he bumped into.

A girl younger than him by maybe a year. Her hair was brown and curly. Innocent green eyes lights up her pale face that had some blemish scars. She had a small face but reminded Cody of a cat with how her eyes were shaped.

"I'm sorry. I spaced out for a moment." Cody apologized.

"It's okay." she said. She stared at him with a strange look but looked away after a second.

Soon the bus pulled up with a shriek of its brakes. The doors open and Cody and the girl got on. They were the first stop on the bus's route so they had the bus to themselves. Cody walked to the last row on the right side of the bus. His usual spot. The girl sat a few rows away but was within earshot.

Cody takes out his phone and earbuds. He was about to put them on when he looks out the window.

Someone was standing outside one of his neighbor's houses. Mr. Takanawa, Cody thought. He didn't know his neighbors closely but recognized their houses and who lived there.

The person stood there completely still like a statue. Taking a close look at the person, Cody could tell it was a male. He wore black jeans and a black jacket, looked to be 5'10. Cody had a photographic memory and could describe the man on point.

Almost as if he felt his eyes, the person turned around. The person's hoodie fell back and revealed fire red hair. The sides of his head was shaven in a buzz and long bangs covered the left half of his face. Cody saw a nose ring on the man's left nostril and could make out a scar at the top of the person's left eyebrow.

Cody noticed that the person could be at least in his early twenties, and his eyes . . . they seemed to glow like sparkling water.

The bus started moving before he knew it. Moving Cody away from that person that seemed to stare directly into his soul. He followed the person with his eyes. Not breaking contact with the man until he was just a speck in the distance.

"What are you looking at?" asked the girl.

It felt like he was broken out of a trance when Cody looked at her. "Nothing. Just spaced out again." he lied. He didn't know what he saw, but for all he knew that guy was just some weirdo.

It took the bus twenty minutes to collect the kids that were on the bus route. Cody didn't pay attention to any of them as they headed toward school. His mind was still on that man. The man gave Cody a creepy vibe with the way the man stared at him. It was like he was staring into his soul.

Cody didn't know what to think, but he had a feeling he may see that person again.

Chapter 3

Adrian

That boy stared at him as if he was studying him. He could feel the boy's eyes as they studied his every detail.

Though the window was in the way, he could see the boy was quite handsome.

Admittedly, the feel of the boy's eyes on him made Adrian smile hotly. He watches as the bus took off, but he could see the boy continue watching him. Could feel his eyes even when the bus drove farther and farther away.

'Admirer?' Adrian thought curiously. He shrugs off the thought and looks back at the task at hand.

The house was small, maybe two stories, not counting the attic. Possibly three or four bedrooms. Two windows stood at the bottom half and three at the top of the house. Adrian could see a latch-door on the roof from where he stood. He spots a security camera hiding in a tree in the form of an owl.

'Silly man.' Adrian thought before he walks straight to the door. Keeping his face away from the camera, he walks up to the door. His hand holds on to the knife hidden in his hoodie pocket. When he was a foot from he door, Adrian peered through the window. No signs of any one.

The knock echoed throughout the house. Adrian listened closely and hears the faint noise of footsteps coming toward him.

The door opens and reveals an older man. He was an Asian man, had grey thinning hair, and wrinkles on his face showing old age. The man was a foot shorter than Adrian but he could see some muscle on him.

"May I help you?" he asked slightly agitated.

"Hello Sir, my name is Michael Rain. I'm here to spread the word of Jesus Christ." Adrian lied as he takes out a book. He pulls his hoodie back to reveal his fire red hair. "Sorry for the lack of formal wear. I was worried about rain." he said.

A skeptic look was on the man's face as he watched Adrian. "I don't have much time. I'm heading to work soon." he said. With a nod, Adrian backs away. "I'm sorry for wasting your time then. Have a good day, Sir." Adrian said kindly as he turns around.

The second the man turns around as he was closing the door, Adrian struck. He spun on his heel and forced his way through the door. His arm hit the door and had it slam against the wall with a bang. The man fell back and tripped on his feet.

"What the hell?!" yelled the man as he gets back to his feet.

A wide, creepy smile grew on Adrian's face. His white teeth were shown and his eyes grew bigger with happiness. "Next time, don't beat your daughter." Adrian said creepily. He takes out his knife as he shuts the door behind him.

Fear appeared in the man's eyes as he starts to back away. Adrian pursued him in a calm walk. "Mr. Takanawa. Widower.

A single daughter. Arrested for child molesting and abuse." Adrian counted off the information he was informed. "What are you talking about?! I never hurt anyone!" Mr. Takanawa defended himself.

"DONT LIE!" Adrian screamed furiously. His mood changed from cheerful to scary. "YOU BEAT YOUR DAUGHTER TILL SHE RAN AWAY!" he screamed. With the speed of lightning, Adrian grabs Mr. Takanawa by the throat and places the knife horizontally of his mouth. He stuffs it farther in till the corners of Mr. Takanawa's mouth started to bleed.

Tears began to fall from Mr. Takanawa's eyes as he cries. He didn't dare move as Adrian starts to ramble.

"You thought you wouldn't be caught. You thought you would get away with it! Defiantly not! I'll be the one to stop you! I'll fucking stop you!"

An evil smile grew on Adrian's face as he watched fear grow more and more on Takanawa's face. The insanity that Adrian showed was clear to Takanawa that he won't be getting out of this alive.

"Now, why don't we walk to the bedroom." Adrian said suddenly. He pulls the knife away and gets off of Takanawa. "Get up." he ordered. The knife was pointed at Takanawa's threat, and Adrian was prepared for any sudden movements. Slowly, Takanawa got back onto his feet and began to walk toward his bedroom.

The walk upstairs was slow and painful. Adrian looked at the pictures hung on the wall. A family of three, all looked happy throughout the years, but he could see the pain in the girl's eyes. The bitterness she felt toward her father. It matched the way Adrian felt for his own farther.

Noticing his lack of concentration, Takanawa attempted a break for it. He ran up the stairs full speed. Only, Adrian was faster. He throws his knife and it hits its mark. The blade sank into the back of Takanawa's head. He stumbled a bit till he fell forward. His head crashing against the wall.

Adrian didn't say anything as he walked to the top of the steps. Blood was already pooling around Takanawa's head. The air was becoming thick with the coppery smell. He stared emotionlessly at the body as he pulls the knife out of his head. "You should always follow the rules. But you never do." Adrian told Takanawa. He puts on leather gloves and grabs Takanawa's arms.

"I wish you were awake. Taking you to the bedroom would be easier." Adrian continued rambling.

The bedroom that was closest was Takanawa's daughter's room. Old drawings and photos still hung on the wall. There were first place ribbons for various sports. Adrian could see the daughter was a true athlete yet she was abused every day.

He tosses Takanawa's body on the bed. The body rolls till it was facing upright. Blood began to soak the bedsheets and pillows. "My, my, aren't you a bleeder." Adrian said with a laugh. He smiled at the body before he walks out of the room. Humming to an unknown tune as he walks downstairs. Blood got on his boots but he didn't seem to mind. Cleaning the knife of blood, he pockets the knife in his jacket.

Adrian didn't leave right away. He looks at the pictures on the walls. A disgusted look was on his face. "There is never a family that is happy." he thought aloud.

Walking to the back of the house, Adrian sees a plate of half eaten breakfast. "Oh, bacon!" he said happily as he snatches a piece of bacon and eats it. "Not bad." he said in between bites.

Chapter 4

C ody

Many police cars drove speedily passed his high school. He watched as they sped away through the window.

It was last period and Cody was in math class. He was slightly out of it because his mind was still on the person he saw. A creepy vibe came from the person but Cody learned not to judge a person right away without getting to know them. Not that he wants to know who that person was.

He looks away from the window and concentrates on math. Carefully listening to his teacher.

As he was writing notes down, a paper ball hit him in the side of the head. Cody didn't react at all and just ignores his tormentors. Perfectly at ease with his bullies despite being bullied all his life.

More balls hit him and it was beginning to become annoying. Keeping his eyes on his paper, when a paper ball was about to hit him, he catches the ball just before it hits him. Then he tosses it in the trash can.

The final bell rung and almost every student hurried out of the room. Cody took his time as he collects his things and packs them into his bag. He is bumped into multiple times in hopes of being tripped by his bullies. Only, he stood still and kept a firm stance.

When he was the last one in the room besides his teacher Mr. Cunning, he finally leaves the room. The entire hallway was full of kids running toward where the bus loop and their cars were. Cody quickly maneuvers his way through the crowd to keep himself from being bumped into.

"Cody! Hold on!"

A hand clasped on Cody's shoulder as someone ran up beside him. He sees it was his only friend Michaela Lavender. Only person that considered him not a target.

"Michaela, I told you that you can't scare me." Cody said with a laugh. He pushes Michaela's hand off his shoulder, and they walk to the buses. "Where were you this morning? You didn't come on to the bus." Cody asked. "I had a dentist appointment." Michaela replied with a smile, showing off her clean white teeth. Rolling his eyes, Cody just laughed at his friend.

They got to their bus that was at the front of the line. The bus was packed with every student that was on its route. Cody and Michaela sat together in a seat that was in the middle of the bus. He got the window seat while Michaela sat beside him.

"How's Izzy doing? I haven't seen that lizard in weeks." Michaela got a sparkly look in her eyes as she spoke of the reptile. "I got claw marks from her this morning." Cody said gruffly. He rubs the scratches he got from Izzy. Slightly wincing at the soft sting.

The bus took off with a powerful rumble in the engine. Cody takes out his earbuds and puts them in. He was about to play some music when Michaela suddenly asks,"Did you hear what happened to Mr. Takanawa?"

The memory of that man flashes across Cody's brain before he asks,"What happened?" He looks at Michaela and saw her usual happiness was gone and was replaced with grim. "He was murdered this morning." she answered.

Shock and horror was on Cody's face at the news. "What do you mean? How is that possible?" he asked in slight terror. His mind kept going back to the man. Whoever that man was, he might be . . .

"My mom called 911 for a noise complaint. Said there was shouting in Mr. Takanawa's house. They went to check and found him dead in his daughter's bed. Apparently he was stabbed in the back of the head." she explained

Michaela fingered her bracelet. "I heard he used to abuse his daughter. Maybe that's why he was killed." she said.

"I saw someone." Cody said suddenly. It caught Michaela by surprise but she looks at him in confusion. "What do you mean?" she asked. "I saw someone standing in front of his house. He seemed very sketchy to me." Cody said, concentrating on the image of the man.

"You think that was the killer?" Michaela asked suggestively. "I don't know. But he gave me a bad vibe." Cody said in a dark tone.

Michaela and Cody's bus stop was almost blocked with all the cop cars. They stepped out and were met with Sarah waiting for them. She had a worried look on her face but it didn't meet her eyes as they were full of tears. Cody knew that Sarah and Mr. Takanawa were good friends because they shared food recipes. His death must be taking a serious toll on her.

"I'll text you later. I gotta make sure my mom isn't going crazy from fear." Michaela said before she ran off.

Cody looked at his foster mother and could tell what she needed. He pulls Sarah into a hug and held on to her till she was resolved to hiccups. "Don't worry, Sarah. Everything will be alright." Cody said, trying to calm her down. He was used to being consoled and knew how to take care of mourning people.

"Lets go home. I'll make something for you." Cody said softly. As he pat her back, he looks up to look at all the police cars. A news crew was standing outside of the Do Not Cross signs. But that didn't catch his attention. Just beyond the crowd was a familiar figure. His clothes were different but Cody recognized his hair.

Replaced with an AC/DC t-shirt and blue jeans. He no longer had a black hoodie but a jean jacket. His hair was longer than Cody had thought. The bangs dangled over his eyes and nearly hid his face.

The man was watching as the police were investigating. For a second, Cody thought he saw pride on the man's face.

"Cody?" Sarah asked when she notices that he was staring off.

"I'll be right back. I'll meet you back home." Cody said before he starts to advance toward the man. Careful to not catch the attention of the person of interest. He was careful not to walk too quickly. One wrong move can alert the man.

No one got in Cody's way as he walked. They were all too busy focusing on the crime scene.

He was almost on top of the person when those familiar blue eyes pierces him in the soul. It felt like he was frozen in place as the man stared at him. Cody felt cold as he was being watched.

Just as he was there, the person was gone. Disappearing when someone walked by in front of Cody. "Shit!" Cody hissed as he looks around. Where did he go? Cody thought angrily.

Chapter 5

Adrian

He sensed the eyes on him before he saw that boy. It felt like fire was burning into the side of his head. Adrian tried to ignore the feeling but it grew and grew till it felt like he had a bell ringing in his head.

When he turns to face the person who was staring at him. He was caught by surprise to find the person was that boy that watched him this morning. 'Shit,' Adrian thought. The eyes on the boy was accusing and questioning. Watching Adrian with a careful look.

Quickly, Adrian slips away in the crowd. He is careful to not catch the attention of anybody.

He hides behind a minivan that was a few feet away. His heart was pounding from the fear of being caught. "That boy . . . He recognized me," Adrian said to himself. Looking through the window of the car, Adrian watches the crowd. Surveying the people and looking for that boy.

There he was. Tall but thin. Dark hair with pale skin. Adrian didn't realize it until now, but the boy was very attractive. Even from a distance, Adrian could see some nice features.

Those eyes could see through anyone. His skin looked soft. His lips looked plump to touch.

Adrian couldn't help but stare at the boy's face. He has never seen someone so attractive. Excitement built up inside of him as he continued to watch the boy.

The boy looked around the crowd, trying to find Adrian. It took Adrian all he had not to just run up to the boy and show him he was there. He didn't understand why he was feeling this way. Sure the boy was quite handsome looking, but it doesn't mean he deserved Adrian's attention. The ones who had Adrian's attention were the ones who needed to be killed.

He watches as the boy gave up on his search and walked away. It felt as if his heart was being pulled away by the boy.

'What is this feeling,' Adrian thought.

Cody

There was no sign of the man anywhere. It irked Cody as he searched for the familiar red head. 'How does a person just disappear like that?!' Cody thought angrily. His eyes scan over the crowd. Careful not to miss a single detail in any person.

Cody runs to the end of the sidewalk and looks around. If he was certain, the man might've hidden somewhere. Maybe where no one would find him. He looks at the houses and cars that were close to him. No one stood out to him. He didn't even see a sign of red hair.

He finally gives up and starts walking back to his house. Some people in the crowd were leaving and heading back to their own houses. Cody looks at the news crew and saw that they were busy reporting. It pissed him off that they were taking advantage of the crime. Not only were they reporting the news, they were using it to get good ratings.

"Oh, excuse me, sir!" called out the newscaster lady.

Cody turns around to see her running toward him. Her business skirt was riding up to her upper thigh, her hair bounced like springs, and her smile seemed to change to a flirtatious one.

"May I help you?" Cody kept his calm and charming tone. Learning to be calm and nice in situations.

"Do you live in this neighborhood? Do you happen to know who the victim is?" she asks, shoving a microphone in Cody's face. At once, Cody's calm demeanor changed to a glare. "I'm not answering questions. Ever heard of privacy?" he snapped.

The smile on the woman's face changed to a frown. "So you're confirming you did know the victim?" she countered.

"Ain't this harassment?" Cody asked coldly before walking passed the woman and the cameraman.

He walked briskly down the sidewalk. Hoping to shake the feeling of being watching. Probably by that news woman.

Sarah wasn't that far ahead of him. She was standing in the middle of the sidewalk, waiting for Cody. Her cheeks were glistening from her tears. The redness in her face was brighter than any red he has seen. Cody has never seen his foster mother cry so much in the years he's known her.

"Sarah, I asked you to go home." Cody said almost softly. He rests a hand on her shoulder and gave it a squeeze. "You shouldn't be here." he said. "One of my friends was murdered. I need to be here." Sarah said insistently.

'Just like me five years ago.' Cody thought. He takes a deep breath and nods. "I know how you feel, Sarah. Losing someone close to you. But being too close is much more damaging." he said.

It seemed like he got to her. She looked back at the scene before she looks back at Cody and nods. "I'm sorry, Cody. You're right, I shouldn't be anywhere near this place." Sarah said.

Giving her an encouraging smile, Cody hugs Sarah tightly. "Lets head home and get something to eat." he said. "Okay." Sarah agreed. Wrapping his left arm around her shoulders, Cody leads Sarah back to the house. Though he could still feel eyes on him as they walked away. He looks over his shoulder, and for a second thought he saw a flash of red.

Chapter 6

Cody

Izzy greeted them like a dog but without the barking. She scurried across the floor and tries to climb up Sarah's legs. Sensing the distress between the two. She successfully climbed up Sarah's body and rests on her shoulder. Despite being big, she was actually light-weight.

"You go sit down on the couch while I'll make some food." Cody ordered. He tries to pick up Izzy but was given a hiss by the reptile.

Quickly pulling his arms away, he frowns at the creature. "Yet you enjoy sleeping with me!" Cody said. He was given a snuffy noise which seemed to resemble a scoffing noise.

Sarah laughed at her pet and cuddled Izzy in her arms. "She hasn't had her fruit yet. She'll feel better after she had her fruit." she said amusingly. She walked off to the living room with Izzy still in her arms. Cody watched them for a moment before heading to the kitchen.

He noticed the kitchen was perfectly clean. Not unusual but it was too clean. Cody knew Sarah enough that when everything is perfectly clean in the house, it meant she was trying to take her mind off of things. Cody rummaged through the cabinets and grabs a pot and wooden spoon. Then he goes through the pantry and grabs the mac-and-cheese mix.

"Hope you're in the mood for mac and cheese because it's the only thing I really know how to make!" Cody called out as he collects water in to the pot. "Extra cheesy please!" Sarah called back. "Got it!" Cody shouted.

The water started to boil sooner than he thought. He dumps the shells in to the water and starts stirring. Once they settled in, he pours the cheese mix. "Should be ready in about five minutes!" he shouted. He hears the familiar clacking of Izzy's claws across the floor as he continues stirring.

Figuring she wanted fruit, he grabs an apple that was lying in a bowl. He takes a knife from its cube and cuts up the apple. Cutting it into pieces small enough for Izzy to chew, Cody puts them on a plate and sets it down on the floor. He saw the familiar green color of her scales and watches as she walks up to the plate. Cody stands back up and continues making mac and cheese. The color and shells became the perfect color and felt soft enough with the spoon.

After turning off the stove, he grabs two bowls from the cabinet above the stove. "The mac and cheese is ready! Come and get it, Sarah!" Cody called in to the living room.

As he collects the mac and cheese into the bowls, Sarah walks into the kitchen. "Here you go." Cody said as he hands Sarah a bowl. "Thank you." Sarah said as she takes the bowl. He notices mascara was smeared all over her face from the tears. Her eyes were redder than before.

Not saying anything, he hands her a spoon before he begins to eat. "Hope its good enough for Chef Sarah Elias." Cody joked as he takes another bite. "Chewy and cheesy. Just how I like it." Sarah said in between chews.

A vibration in Cody's pocket alerted him of a text message. He sets his bowl down and takes out his phone. It was a text from Michaela.

Can we talk?NOW!

Confused for a second, he texts back.

Wanna come over?

Almost immediately she responds.

No. At the tree. Please.

Cody stared at his phone for a second before stuffing it back in his jeans. "Michaela wants to talk. Is it okay if I leave for a few minutes?" Cody asked. He didn't want to leave Sarah by herself, but he learned never to dismiss Michaela when she has news.

"It's fine. I have Izzy to comfort me." Sarah said as she rubs the reptile's head. "I can't believe this is normal for me." Cody thought aloud, earning himself a laugh from Sarah. He takes one last bite of his mac-and-cheese before leaving the house.

Exiting the house, he went left, going up the sidewalk. He walks uphill and heads toward the neighborhood park. The air had gotten colder then this morning. Cody could see his breath each time he breathed. Goosebumps ran up his arms despite being in a leather jacket.

The walk to the park wasn't long, just about a quarter of a mile. Kids don't usually go to the park when it was October where he used to live, but he didn't know much about the kids here. New York was still a new place to him.

"Cody! Over here!" called out Michaela.

He looks passed the jungle gym and saw Michaela in a big oak tree. She was hanging upside down on a large branch. Already she changed out of her clothes and wore skinny jeans and a crop top that pressed against her skin to keep from drifting up. Cody laughed at her clothes and inability of her being cold. He walks to the tree and was eye to eye with Michaela.

"You know that you could fall, right?"

"I've been doing this for years. I'll be fine." Michaela said as she slowly unhooked herself from the tree. She flips midair and lands flat on her feet. "Enough with showing off." Cody said with a fake whine. "Why did you call me here?" he asked.

"Police sent investigators to our house and other neighbors. They found video cam footage in that owl statue Takanawa had. They didn't go into specifics but said that there was a man that visited him probably an hour before he died." Michaela explained. She takes out a piece of paper from her jacket pocket and unfolds it. "They showed us a picture but we couldn't see his face." she said as she handed Cody the picture. "Was this the guy you saw?" she asked.

Cody takes the picture and looks at it. He takes a short intake of breath. It was the guy he saw, no doubt about it. He recognized the clothes and the person matched the height. The picture was in full color but there weren't any defining features on the person other than their clothes and height.

"Same clothes. It has to be." Cody shortened his answer. He didn't want to think about possibly seeing a murderer. If he just reported the suspicious activity or something, Mr. Takanawa might still be alive. There was just one thing that doesn't make sense.

Why was he killed in the first place?

"It's freaking my mom out. She's afraid there's a serial killer on the loose. There was a murder last week. A lady in her mid-forties was found dead with a stab wound in her neck." Michaela didn't go into specifics but didn't have to. Cody could already imagine it. "That could be nothing. Even if it was the same person, wouldn't there have to be a connection?" Cody asked. He knew that Michaela was a horror-chick. She was in criminal investigation at school and was top of her class.

"Of course. For all we know Mr. Takanawa had something that sent this killer after him." Michaela started stating facts of famous killers that had certain ideas in their victims and what they wore. It made Cody just tune her out and look around them as she talked. His eyes look over to the swing set and his breath was cut short.

There he stood.

That fire red hair brightened the area that was full of grey. He stood underneath a tree behind the swing set. Those ice blue eyes stared directly at Cody.

Cody felt coldness flood into his body as he stared back at the man. Fear built up inside.

"Cody? Are you okay?" Michaela asked worriedly. She was about to look at what Cody was looking at but was grabbed by the shoulder. "Don't turn around," Cody hissed. "He's watching." he added, not breaking eye contact with Him.

Michael's eyes were now full of terror. She tried to look without moving her head but Cody kept her from doing so. Cody forced her to turn around, and they start to walk away. "Don't look or try anything brave." Cody said in her ear. She gives him a short nod.

He could feel the eyes of their stalker on him. Cody wrapped an arm around Michaela's shoulder and pressed her close to his side. Scared that she might be yanked from him like every loved one.

Chapter 7

Adrian

It felt like fire was burning in his chest as he watched the boy walk off with the girl. He wished he had the ability to kill a person with a glare as he stared at the girl's head. His jealousy didn't stop when the boy wrapped his arm around her.

Adrian slips away from his hiding place and began to follow them. He takes off his jacket and turns it inside out. The inside was red and there were pockets on the inside. He puts the jacket back on and throws the hoodie over his head.

He keeps a twenty feet distance from the two. His eyes were staring at the ground but his senses were trained on them.

As the wind blew his way, Adrian hears parts of their conversation.

"Is he following . . . should we run?" spoke the girl.

A low growl rumbled in Adrian's throat. He wanted to jam a knife down the girl's throat. Turn her throat inside out and see if she could still speak.

The boy turned his head and looked directly at Adrian. For some unknown reason, Adrian felt chills run down his spine.

The boy's eyes were cold and full of hatred. There wasn't a hint of fear in those brown orbs.

Adrian stopped walking and just stared. The two walked away, and Adrian wished that the boy would stop to look at him. The couple turned the corner and was no longer in his view. Instead of following them, he turns around and walks back to the park. He walks to the swing set and sits down. Memories began to flood his mind as a bitter feeling filled his heart.

He swung high above the bars of the swing set as he was being pushed by his father. Laughter came out of him as he felt as if he was flying. "Higher, Daddy!" called out seven year-old Adrian.

His father laughed as he pushes harder. "Can't go too high or you'll fly off." his father told him. "I want to fly!" Adrian said. He kicks his legs as he swings. His brown hair flies in his face but he didn't care.

Adrian prepares to jump off. He has a determined look on his face as he stared forward; however, it disappears when he sees his mom.

She was sitting on a bench with a man, and they were kissing. Her hands were on the man's face while his were on her waist. Adrian often saw that interaction between his parents. Not with other people.

He doesn't realize he lost his grip on the swing till he slips off. Letting out a cry, Adrian went sailing and landed on his stomach. Pain ruptured his stomach as he starts to sit up. Tears begin to form in his eyes and he started to cry.

"Adrian! Are you okay?" asked his father as he ran up to Adrian. Adrian continued to cry as he sat up, holding his stomach in pain. "M-Mommy was k-kissing another m-man!" Adrian whimpered as he wipes his eyes. He looked up at his father and saw shock in his eyes. Then he looked up and peered through the park, searching for Adrian's mom.

That day was the start of a new but terrible life. Adrian growled as he remembered the beatings his father gave him after his mom left. He took them all, believing he was to blame. That is till that night that he had enough.

A thrilling pleasure shot through Adrian as he recalled the night he murdered his father. It felt like he was in ecstasy as Adrian stabbed him. He wished he could do it again.

His apartment was small and drafty. The walls were a pale tan color with cracks in the foundation. Adrian was able to clean some of the odd stains that were left from the previous owners. (He was considering the last owners were party people.)

There was only a couch and a small tv in the living room. The setting sun was peaking through the balcony window. Adrian enjoyed the sunset because it meant that a new world opens up when the night comes. The night was his day and the day was his night.

Throwing off his hoodie, he tosses it on the couch along with his shirt. On his pale and lean chest was the word 'psycho' written in cursive. It curved downwards just below the collar bone. Adrian had gotten the tattoo when he was seventeen. Just after his second kill.

The cold air barely phased his skin. He didn't get goosebumps or chills. Instead he feels a soft shiver of delight. He had gotten used to the cold after being on the run from the police. Now the cold gave him a certain thrill.

He walks into what could barely be described as a bedroom. There was only a duffle bag for his clothes and he hadn't set up the bed yet. For a week he has been sleeping on a mattress that laid on the floor.

"Home sweet home." Adrian scoffed. He falls ungracefully on the mattress and buries his face in the pillow. Closing his eyes, he tries to fall asleep and forget about the boy.

Didn't work.

The boy's face was stuck in his mind. Those brown eyes that pierced Adrian's soul like a knife. His face didn't show any signs of blemishes but had a few scars that looked to be from a bad past. (He had his fair share of scars from his past that may be relatable.)

Adrian let out a yell of frustration and throws himself up into a sitting position. His bangs covered his eyes as he glared at his hands.

'That boy . . . he obviously recognized me. No doubt he will tell the police. I can't let that happen.' he thought with a clench of his fists. He gets off his bed and walks to the closet. There was chainlink lock and another lock that needed a key. Adrian takes off his necklace that held the key. He slips the key in and unlocks both locks.

The closet doors open and reveal a wall full of weapons. The wall that faced Adrian had many knives and daggers he collected over the years. At the bottom were guns that had silencers attached.

A stoic look was on Adrian's face as he looks over his weapons. He grabs a dagger with a wooden hilt and a black blade with sharp teeth poking out at the end. He could feel it begging for the taste of blood.

'Soon. I'll get to see that cute face of yours as it contorts in pain.' A creepy smile grew on his face as he thought of killing another person.

Chapter 8

C ody

Sweat ran down Cody's body as he pulls up on the bar for the fiftieth time. His face felt like it was on fire and his arms were screaming for release. He bites down on his lip to try and give him some energy through pain.

'Ten more.' Cody thought with a hiss of air.

His chin touches the top of the bar; and he couldn't do it anymore. Cody falls on the ground ungracefully. A heavy grunt escaped him as he lands on the floor. "Son of a bitch," he growled.

Closing his eyes, he tries to catch his breath. He has been going to the gym and doing pull-ups to cope with his parents' death. At first, he had counseling but it didn't work out. So now he does fitness to help get rid of conflicting emotions.

A familiar clacking sound entered his room and headed toward him. He turns his head to the right to be face to face with Izzy. The large lizard stared at him with big eyes and breathed in his face. "You know no boundaries, do you?" Cody asked sarcastically.

Izzy doesn't say anything but crawls on top of Cody's bare chest. She settles in to a big ball and seems to fall asleep.

The most weirdest look was on Cody's face as he looks at the iguana. He didn't know whether to just lay there and let her sleep or try and get up and risk a scratching. Made that mistake once, not letting that happen again.

As he lays there, he thinks of what happened in the afternoon. He knew that that man was following him and Michaela. His instincts were on alert and was prepared for anything. Only Cody hadn't seen the man when he dropped off Michaela or when he walked back home. He wanted to tell Michaela but was afraid to scare her. Despite acting like she wasn't afraid of anything, she can become terrified.

His back began to become sore from the hard ground. He dared to move only an inch to get comfortable. Izzy let out a growl in her sleep, making Cody freeze. "One. Two. Three." he counted before quickly rotating his body. The iguana falls on the floor and Cody quickly bolts away from her. It took him a split second to jump on his bed before he could get caught by Izzy's tail.

"Missed me," Cody yelled in triumph. "Take that, Izzy!" he finished with a finger pointed at Izzy. She glared at him in what would be described as a tired frown. With a huff, she scuttles off like a beetle out of the room.

Never before in his life did he feel relieved. He rubs his ankles absentminded, recalling the many whippings Izzy would give him. She didn't trust him the first time they met. It took at least a month for her to finally trust him. He never had a pet before so it was a first to have an iguana snuggle against him.

Taking in a deep breath, he turns off his bedside lamp before laying down on his bed. He would've taken a shower but it was almost midnight and he was too tired. Closing his eyes, he slowly begins to fall asleep.

Suddenly, he hears a creak. His body went rigid and he opens his left eye. Already adjusted to the darkness, Cody examines his room. The creaking continued slowly, coming from the window. Cody knew to always have his window locked so whoever was there unlocked it themselves. There was one thing that unsettled him most. He was on the second floor and there wasn't a tree or even a ladder near his window.

The familiar sound of the window opening fully resonated across the room. Cody's breathing became shallow and fear from deep within began to surface. The memories of the home invasion filled his thoughts. It took all he had not to cry.

Two thumps that would've been silent unless it was for his trained ears. A shadow moved on the wall toward Cody. He squints his eyes to appear asleep while he watched the intruder walked toward him.

A tall figure stood in front of him. The person was close enough that Cody could smell them. A thick cologne that smelled of spice and cinnamon. Cody slowly looked up and had to catch himself from gasping.

It was him.

Through the darkness, Cody could see those cold blue eyes gleaming at him. He could tell something was in his hand. The man raises his arm up, and Cody could see it was a large knife. It was face down, the tip of the blade aiming toward Cody's head.

The man throws down his hand, but Cody jumps out of the way. Throwing himself at the killer and tackling him to the ground, Cody wraps his hands around his neck and begins to strangle the killer. "I know who you are! You fucking killed Takanawa!" Cody growled. Cody got on top of him and started to wrestle the man for the knife.

Growls escaped the killer as he uses his weight to throw Cody off of him. "I may have killed him but he deserved it!" he hissed in Cody's ear. He presses all his weight against Cody's chest to keep him from moving. Cody tries to fight him but stops when he feels the coolness of the blade against his throat. Sharp points dug into his skin like teeth.

"Not so tough now are you?" asked the killer. He straddled Cody's hips to keep him on the ground. One hand was pressed against Cody's head while the other held the knife. "I am impressed you were able to fight me," he said impressed. A cruel smile was on his face as he stared at Cody. He runs his fingers down Cody's cheek with surprisingly sharp nails.

Cody doesn't say anything as he watched him. "Why did you kill him? Who are you?" he asked. It felt like he was staring death in the face. In which he might be . . .

"Since this is your last day, I'll answer your questions. My name's Adrian. I won't tell you my last name." said the killer.

The sound of his voice so close and so calm . . . it sent exciting chills down Cody's spine. "That Takanawa fellow abused his daughter. Sometimes I am hired by people to kill. Only I decide who I kill, depends on what they've done."

Adrian said. He takes in a deep breath and leans forward to be just inches away from Cody's face. "Takanawa had it coming. His daughter found me and asked me to kill him. I saw the scars on her. I didn't take her money out of pity." he said in a whisper.

He's killed before . . . he doesn't care . . . Cody thought in horror.

"Why are you trying to kill me?" Cody asked meekly. He didn't wish to speak but had to try and stall Adrian.

A smile grew on Adrian's face that was almost warm. "You obviously recognize me. I can't have witnesses." he said in a bitter tone. His lips ghosted across Cody's lips. "Too bad. You are very cute." he whispered. The knife began to dig into Cody's skin. Close to breaking his flesh.

Without thinking, Cody grabs Adrian's shoulders and throws himself on top of him. Adrian's grip on the knife was loose so Cody was able to snatch it. He presses the knife into Adrian's throat and smirks triumphantly at him. "If you weren't trying to kill me, I would be flattered." Cody said almost sadistically.

Their eyes were locked on each other. One showed anger and fear. The other showed . . . lust.

Suddenly, Cody was pulled forward and found himself being kissed. Adrian forced his tongue inside of Cody's mouth. His hand was holding the back of Cody's head to keep him from moving. An arm wraps around Cody's waist and pulls him to be pressed against Adrian's chest.

'Fuck! Fuck! Fuck!' Cody thought as he fought Adrian.

The need for air came over the both of them and they break away. Cody pushes off of Adrian and scoots away from him. The knife was still in his hand and he kept it pressed against his chest. "What the hell was that?!" Cody demanded angrily.

A fake innocent look was on Adrian's face. "I wanted to know what you tasted like." he replied. He crawls toward Cody on his hand and knees. "Stay back!" Cody ordered, holding out the knife in front of him. "I'll fucking stab you!" he threatened.

Instead of being afraid, Adrian nudges the knife away from his face. He was just a foot away from Cody. "You aren't going to hurt me." he whispered before kissing Cody again.

Chapter 9

C ody

Screams of bloody murder echoed all over the house. Gunshots shook the walls. Angry yells from unfamiliar voices sent violent chills down twelve year old Cody's spine. He covers his ears to try and muffle the sound, but it was futile as he hears the intruders' demand for money.

They came in so quick. He was about to go to bed after watching a movie with his parents. His mother gave him a glass of water when they burst through the door guns blazing.

There were five guys. They wore ski masks and wore all black. The guns they had were huge. It was like looking at a scary movie up close, except it was real life. Cody's mother leads Cody away from the men as his father confronts them. His father was a policeman and was prepared for them with a gun of his own.

Gunshots fired and flew above Cody and his mother's head. He let out a scream as his ears popped from the close range of the gun fire. His mother held him close as they ran to the basement door.

"Go downstairs and hide in the corner. Don't come out until me or your father comes for you." his mother ordered as she opens the door and ushers Cody downstairs. "But what about-" Cody was cut off when his mother shut the door. He didn't go after her; he follows her orders and runs downstairs.

The gunshots were muffled and the shouts grew louder. His mother's voice joined the shouts. He had never heard her so mad but could hear the fear as well.

Cody hides in a dark corner behind the water heater. He curls up in a ball and tucks his head between his knees. It sounded like a war was going on upstairs. But who was winning?

A trickle of urine runs down his pants as fear filled him. Fear gripped him in a vise grip.

Suddenly, everything became quiet. Utterly still. Cody couldn't breathe as he waits for a sound. Any sound. His heart began to pound harder and harder as the suspense grew. The quietness seemed to grow louder and louder.

His eyes shot open when his alarm started blaring in his ear. His body jolted awake in surprise. Sweat covered him like a blanket. Cody felt like he was on fire but at the same time was cold. He slowly sits up on his bed, craning his neck around to stretch it. Pain shot through his neck like needles.

Grabbing his throat, Cody feels something dry and puffed up on his neck. He crawls off his bed and walks to the mirror. What greeted him made him choke up.

A line of dry blood ran across his throat. Bruise marks surrounded the mysterious cut shaped like finger prints.

Cody recalls what he thought was a dream. Everything started to come back to him. The rush of adrenaline and fear he felt as he fought the killer . . . and the kiss.

His face became completely flushed. The familiar feel of the killer–Adrian's–lips came back to him. He couldn't deny it, but the touch of Adrian's lips was amazing. And it was his first kiss.

He didn't realize he slapped himself till the sting of it grew on his face. 'What the hell are you thinking?! He tried to kill you and killed Mr. Takanawa!' Cody's thoughts screamed at him. But why didn't Adrian kill him last night . . .

"Cody? Are you up?" called out Sarah. Hearing her voice made him sigh in relief. At least she wasn't murdered, he thought. "I'm up." Cody replied but his voice was hoarse. He coughed to try and clean his throat but it instead strained it more. "I'll be down in a minute." he said with another cough.

Cody steps back to open his dresser drawer when he steps on something cold and thin that made a clink sound. He looks down, and shivers shot up his spine. Underneath his foot was the knife Adrian tried to kill him with. It somehow gleamed in the low light coming from the window. The edge of the blade was darker from the blood is no doubt had stained on it.

All of a sudden, he felt very sick. His digested dinner started to come up in a rush. Quickly, he runs out of his room and to the bathroom. Saliva ran down his mouth just as he lost control of the contents. He barely made it to the toilet as he lost all contents in his stomach. It wasn't quick nor pleasant.

When his stomach finally settled, Cody felt twenty pounds lighter. His legs were weak and his arms were heavy. 'I hate my life,' he thought.

"Cody?" Sarah spoke.

Cody doesn't look up because he felt a second rush and vomits up stomach fluid. "Busy." he said in between gasps. He feels his back being rubbed as Sarah consoled him. "Want me to get you some water?" she asked concerned. "Yes please." Cody said as his stomach finally settled.

Taking in a slow deep breath, Cody stood back up. He realizes that Sarah had left, probably to get him water. Izzy was resting by the door, watching him with annoyance. (Probably for the night before.)

"Don't give me that look. Try being me last night." Cody snapped at the iguana before grabbing his toothbrush. He begins to scrub his mouth and get rid of the horrible taste of digested food and stomach acid out of his mouth. He looks at himself in the mirror and saw a sickly reflection. The look of him could make people cringe. 'That bastard better not be the cause of this.' Cody thought angrily.

Sarah reenters the bathroom with a glass of water. She hands Cody the water as she checks his forehead with the other hand. "You're running a fever and you're red in the face." she stated half of what Cody knew. He feels his cheek but didn't feel that warm. Just cool. "You're staying home today." Sarah stated. "No doubt about it."

There was no reason to argue. Cody felt like crap and he knew it. "Got it." he said as he takes a few sips of water. "Sadly, I have to go to work." Sarah said with a sigh. She picks up Izzy and carries her downstairs as Cody follows Sarah. "I'll be fine by myself. I'm seventeen, I can take care of myself." he said. "Just don't vomit on the carpet." Sarah said half-joking-half serious.

Sarah left around nine because the restaurant, Wolfgang's, opened at 11 for lunch and so forth. At first, she didn't want to leave because she wanted to take care of Cody. After a thirty minute conversation of reasons to trust him, she finally agreed.

She was still shaken from Takanawa's death. It worried Cody and made him consider if he should tell her about Adrian. And the fact he nearly killed Cody while she slept. He decided against it as she collected her keys for her BMW and left.

Without an empty stomach, Cody decided to be productive in his sick state. Retreating to his room to finish some home-work, Cody stopped at the doorway of his bedroom. There the knife laid where it originally was where he found it.

The memory of nearly being slitted by that very weapon made him feel like he might throw-up again. He fingers the bruises on his throat. Slightly confused when Sarah didn't notice them.

Izzy trotted in between his legs. She entered his room and stopped right in front of the knife. A soft growl rumbles in her flappy throat as she sniffed it. Cody smiled at her because she senses the evilness in the scent. It gave him a mental image of Adrian facing off with Izzy. Even if that guy was a killer, a mad Izzy is nothing you want to see.

Then suddenly, she turns toward the closet, a threatening growl escaping through an open mouth. Showing two sets of teeth. That caught Cody's attention as she moved toward his closet. The small spikes on her back stood on end that meant she was in defensive mode.

Cody remained silent as he slowly steps into his room. He bends down and grabs the knife. "Izzy." he hissed in between his teeth. Trying to beckon her with his voice. It didn't work but Izzy backed off a little.

Now standing in front of his closet, Cody prepared for what may be lurking inside. He raises the knife in front of him as he reaches for the knob. 'One. Two. Three.' he counted as he pulls the door open. He was prepared for something to jump out at him. Something to probably attack him. But no . . .

His scared but stern look changed to a weird one. His eyebrows scrunch together and his upper lip moved upward. What he discovers is not only Adrian . . . but a SLEEPING Adrian.

There the killer laid on the floor, resting his head on a pile of clothes. He looked peaceful and not killer-like.

Cody just lost it . . .

"WHAT THE FUCK!"

Chapter 10

Adrian

Everything was pleasant as he slept. He was dreaming of a peaceful scene in a meadow and living in a cabin. With a nice lover that greeted him in bed. It made him smile in his sleep.

"WHAT THE FUCK!"

The yell shocked him into waking up. He jolted up into a sitting position. Letting out a yelp when he feels a crick in his neck. "I should've taken a pillow." he mumbled as he looked up.

The look on the boy's face was hilarious. His face was bright red, his eyebrows knotted together, and his mouth looked like a messed up form of a growl. His hair was tousled from sleep and he looks tired. Almost sickly.

"Oh hey." Adrian said casually. He stretches out his arms and feels them pop.

"Hey?! That's what you fucking say after nearly killing me and sleeping in my damn closet?!"

"Ever heard of forgive and forget?" Adrian asked as he stood up. "No way in hell am I forgiving nor am I fucking forgetting!" exclaimed the boy. He aimed the knife at Adrian's chest with a shaky hand. "Do you kiss your mother with that mouth?" Adrian asked unafraid. He pushes the knife aside like he was brushing away dust and exited the closet. Nearly stepping on a giant lizard.

His ankles were assaulted with its tail. It felt like a whip made of metal wrapped around his ankles. "Shit!" Adrian jumped away from the lizard but it started following him. "Get 'em, Izzy!" ordered the boy. Adrian jumps on the bed before he could be hit again. He peered over the edge and saw the lizard was trying to climb up.

"She doesn't like intruders. Better leave. And never come back." said the boy. He had a smirk on his face as he crossed his arms. "Oh come on. I didn't kill you! Shouldn't that speak for itself?" Adrian asked. "Oh shut up! Just be glad I haven't called the cops yet!" The boy stopped shouting and started coughing. The redness in his face reminded Adrian of a person being strangled.

Slowly, Adrian climbs out of the bed and reaches out to touch him. "Are you alright . . ." he trailed off because he realized that he didn't know the boy's name. 'God, it's a one night stand all over again,' Adrian thought with a cringe.

"Cody."

Adrian looked down at the boy, surprised when he spoke. "What was that?" he asked. "My name is Cody." said the boy. He looked up at Adrian with a teary face from all the coughing. "You already know my face so what does it matter." he said.

His face felt like it was on fire when Cody stared into his eyes. "Are you still afraid?" Adrian asked in almost a whisper. He wanted to kiss that face again without being fought.

"Yes. I'm just wondering why haven't you killed me?" Cody said. He holds the knife up and lightly places it on Adrian's cheek. "Why aren't you afraid of me killing you?" Cody asked. Adrian smiled and takes the knife out of Cody's hand. "You're afraid of hurting people. You couldn't hurt anyone." he said as he stared into Cody's eyes. There was innocence in those brown orbs but something else lurked inside them. He leans in to kiss Cody but only kisses him on the forehead. Cody's skin was hot to the touch on his lips. It was like he was touching fire.

Cody suddenly backs away. He brushes passed Adrian and lays down on his bed. Adrian does a double-take when he saw the iguana was resting on the bed as well. "Your mother must be cool to let you have a pet iguana." Adrian commented. He reaches out to pet Izzy but was hissed at.

"Mmmm nnnhh mmm mmm mmhhh." Cody spoke in muffles. "Huh?" Adrian said confused.

With a grunt, Cody rolls onto his side. "She's not my real mom. She's my foster mother." he said sadly. He runs his fingers over Izzy's back and massaged the back of her neck. "My mother and father passed away in a home invasion." Cody said.

Surprise appeared on Adrian's face. He would've never guessed Cody was an orphan. "I lost my father and mother too," Adrian started. "Except my mom left us and I killed my father." he finished with a laugh. Cody's face turned from sad to a disgusted face. "I'm not going to even ask why. Past is in the past." Cody said as he rubs his temple.

It took all Adrian had to not laugh. Most would be disturbed, yet Cody doesn't seem to care. Not like most people would.

"Cute and carefree. I like that in a boy." Adrian smirked. If it weren't for Cody's already red face, he could've been able to tell he was blushing. "I'm not into boys! And I sure as hell not into killers!" Cody snapped. His yell woke up Izzy from her nap, and she jumps off the bed and scuttles away. The two men watch her as she walked away as if this was any normal day.

Adrian looks back at Cody but was whacked in the chest. "I want you out of here!" Cody demanded angrily. He continued shoving Adrian till they were in the hallway. "I won't tell the cops who you are as long as you don't come back!" he promised with a crack in his voice. Adrian's heart seemed to make a hurtful twist at Cody's words. He narrows his eyes at Cody as he was being shoved to the front door.

"Why must I leave? I find you interesting!" Adrian exclaimed.

"Id be flattered if you didnt try to fucking kill me and weren't a fucking killer!" Cody yelled as he opened the door and shoves Adrian out the door. "Now get the hell away from here!" he yelled before slamming the door in Adrian's face.

The door was so close to his face, he nearly got hit. Adrian blinked a few times as he stared at the door. "So hard to get." he said with a sigh. Turning around, he walks down the front steps and begins to walk down the sidewalk.

Only to stop and turn around to face the house. "Don't think this is the last of you seeing me, Cody." Adrian spoke as if he was talking to Cody directly. He smirks darkly before leaving.

Chapter 11

C ody

The entire day was full of paranoia.

Cody checked and rechecked the windows and doors. He kept Sarah's baseball bat close in case Adrian decided to visit again.

His phone rang many times from Sarah and Michaela. He didn't bother answering them because his mind was boggling with Adrian. It confused him when Adrian didn't try to kill him. He had the chance when Cody fell unconscious. Instead, Adrian puts him back in his bed and slept in the closet.

It took all Cody had not to just yell. He grabbed his hair and yanked it. Hard.

'I hate my life,' he thought angrily. 'Why the hell did I say I wouldn't call the police? He has to be locked away!'

All of a sudden, the doorbell rang. The sound startled Cody since it was the only noise he has heard in awhile. He looks at the door and tries to peer through the stained glass from where he sat on the couch. The doorbell rang again two more times. This time impatiently.

With a shaky breath, Cody stands up and walks to the door. The bat was hidden behind his back and held in a death grip.

He reaches the door but doesn't open it yet. Through the glass he could see two figures. One was smaller and the other taller. He still kept his guard up as he opens the door.

To his surprise, Cody discovers that figures were two policemen. They wore blazers and dress pants but had badges on their chests. The smaller one had black hair styled with a buzzcut, a five o'clock shadow and bushy eyebrows. The other cop had shaggy brown hair and a scar on his eyebrow.

"May I help you?" Cody asked, setting the bat off to the side. "Yes, is Ms. Elias here?" asked Bushy Eyebrows. "No. She's at work." Cody replied. He had a feeling where this was going. "Are you here because of Mr. Takanawa?" he asked without thought.

The cops share a look before Shaggy says," Yes it is. I'm Detective Jackson and this is my partner Detective Johns. We came here because we learned that Ms. Elias is friends with Mr. Takanawa and we wanted to ask her a few questions." He looked passed Cody to see if Sarah would just magically appear. "May I ask who you are?" Detective Jackson asked. "I'm Cody Winters. Sarah is my foster mother." Cody said.

Detective Johns started jotting down notes. It reminded Cody of the night when police officers questioned him about that night. He could still remember the questions.

'Do you know who might've wanted to hurt your parents?'

'Did you see their faces?'

It made Cody want to punch those officers in the face. Didn't they understand that he knew nothing and he just wanted to grieve?

"Did you know Mr. Takanawa?" asked Detective Johns. He had that judging look that said he did not trust Cody. "Not personally. He's visited time to time but I never really talked to him." Cody said, trying not to give Johns the same look. His experience with police has never been great.

"Do you have any reason to believe why Mr. Takanawa was killed?" Johns asked. "Rumor has it that he abused his daughter. At least, that's what I heard." Cody recalls what Adrian had told him. He killed Takanawa because his daughter hired Adrian. She hated her father so much that she hired a psychopath to kill him.

Johns wrote through two pages with unknown notes. Cody tries to see what he wrote but he couldn't understand Johns's handwriting. So he looks at Jackson and asks,"Do I have to call Sarah and tell her you need to talk to her?"

"We would appreciate it. We'll come back tomorrow to talk to her." Jackson said. He grabs Johns's arm and gestures to him to head back to the car. "If you have anything else to tell us, here's my card." Jackson takes out a card from his jacket and hands it to Cody. "Will do." Cody said with a nod and fake smile. With a nod, Jackson leaves with Johns and they drive away from the house.

When they were out of sight, Cody crumples the card and tosses it into a bush. 'Like I'd tell a cop anything', he thought. He closes the front door and walks back into the living room. His spot on the couch was occupied by Izzy, who picked up her head to look at him. "No need to worry, Izzy. Just stupid policemen." Cody assured her as he sat down beside the reptile.

He closes his eyes to try and relax. But his mind was active with the thought of hurting those cops from his past. They dismissed the case after a week with no leads. It angered Cody as he was told this by the social worker. He has never been able to trust anyone that was involved with the police ever since.

His mind wanders to Adrian. That man went above the law and does what he wants. Goosebumps ran up his arms when he thought of all the kills Adrian must have committed. All of the bloodshed. And he could've been one of those kills.

A ding on his phone surprised him. Cody picks up his phone and checks it. A text from Michaela

Are you dead or just sick?

Oh, Michaela, always so worried, Cody thought with a small laugh.

Just sick, he replied.

"Who're you texting?"

Cody let out the most loudest scream when someone spoke behind him. He threw his phone up in the air and it hit the ceiling. "Shit!" he yelled as he jumps off the couch and turns around with his bat swinging at the intruder.

Chapter 12

C ody

The bat nearly hit Sarah in the face if she hadn't ducked in time. She lets out a surprised yelp and drops down to the floor. The bat swung where her head was, making a quick whistle sound as it sliced through the air. "What the hell!" she yelled.

"Shit!" Cody yelled as he drops the bat. "Are you okay? I didn't mean too!" he started rambling in worry. His face was growing hot from embarrassment but felt cold from fear.

Sadly, it wasn't the first time he's done something to almost hurt his foster family. The trauma he experienced had made him cautious with everything. He used to constantly jump and attack things when startled. Sending him to many different orphan homes.

Fear gripped him tightly at the thought of harming Sarah. Once again his fears and paranoia got the best of him

Cody jumps over the couch and helps Sarah back to her feet. "I'm fine. I didn't mean to startle you." Sarah said but looked shaken up. "What's with the bat?" she asked. "I felt safe with it." Cody said in a mumble. He handed her the bat but she doesn't take it. "Can you explain to me why you nearly whacked me with it?" she asked skeptically.

"Police came by. They wanted to talk to you." Cody said, hoping to change the subject. That seemed to catch her attention. "How come?" she asked. "It was about Mr. Takanawa. They said they would come back tomorrow to talk to you." Cody said, now wishing he hadn't thrown away Jackson's card. He could've just given it to Sarah.

A brooding look appeared on Sarah's face. "I still can't believe he's gone. Who would've wanted to kill him?" she asked rhetorically. Oh, if you just knew, Cody thought. "I don't know. Lets just hope he's in a better place." Cody said, feeling so corny when he said that. Many people say that, but who knows where they actually go.

"How come you came home early?" Cody asked confused. He knew for a fact that Sarah doesn't come home till passed midnight. Coming home early is a rarity. Especially in the afternoon.

"I couldn't focus so my boss allowed me to have the rest of the day off. I'll be back tomorrow." Sarah sets her purse on the couch and collects Izzy in her arms. "How was your day? Boring?" she asked expectantly. "Other than the police. Pretty boring." Cody lied. Sarah gave him a suspicious look as if she knew he was lying. She opens her mouth, but Cody was saved when the door rings. "I'll get it!" he said quickly before literally running to the door.

He stops at the door to take a quick breath to calm himself down. Then he opens the door.

A tall man in a grey business suit stood there. He had brown hair with grey streaks in it. His eyes were a soft green and he had thin lines of age on his forehead. His left ear had a tear on the shell that looked like he was slashed at by a knife. Cody noticed a Rolex on his right wrist and a golden chain necklace with the cross attached. The look of him showed a successful man.

"May I help you?" Cody asked, silently hoping this wasn't some detective or something.

"Are you Cody Winters?" the man asked.

Everything became utterly cold inside Cody when he heard his voice. His bones freeze till he was as still as stone. "Y-Yes." he stuttered. His eyes started to grow wide as his memory got to him.

"I'm Michael Winters. I'm your uncle." the man introduced himself.

He was one of the fucking invaders! Cody's mind screamed. Terror built up in his body as he stepped back. "I don't have an uncle. My parents never told me." he denied the fact. That man's voice was the same as the lead intruder from that night. The screams were loud and gruff, but he recognized the voice anywhere.

"Your father and I never got along much, but I assure you that I am your uncle." Michael said with a kind smile.

Before Cody could reply, he sensed a presence behind him. He turns his head to the right and saw Sarah. She still held Izzy and was looking at Michael in confusion. "May I help you?" she asked the same question Cody asked. "Hello, Ms.

Elias. I'm Michael Winters, and as I just said, I'm Cody's uncle." Michael reintroduced himself.

Shock appeared on Sarah's face. "Wouldn't have the social workers known about you then?" she asked a little suspiciously. "My brother didn't write myself in his will as guardian." Michael answered with a saddened look. "I hoped to take care of Cody but couldn't find him," he said.

A bitter feeling settled into Cody's stomach. No way will he believe this man's shit. His parents never told him he had an uncle. And there is no damn way he'll believe some stranger.

"No disrespect sir, but I don't believe you. If I've never heard of you from my parents or even the social workers. How can I believe you?" Cody questioned rather coldly. His eyes scanned Michael's face, memorizing the man's face and wondering if he was really one of them.

Michael looked at Cody in the eye. "I know it's hard to believe but I have proof that I am indeed your uncle." he said as he reaches into the inside pocket of his jacket and takes out a papers. He hands them to Cody, and he takes them reluctantly. Cody unfolds the papers and began reading.

The first page was of his father's family tree. At the very end was his father's and Michael's name. And Cody's. He recognized his grandparents' names above his father's name.

The second page was his father's will. It was written in his father's cursive handwriting. The sight of it made Cody smile. He begins to read the will and was surprised to see his inheritance.

One million dollars.

"Holy shit."

Chapter 13

A drian

He continuously sharpens his knives. Each stroke he made became harder and harder. His eyes were hard and didn't break from what he was doing. Some dust flew off the blade from the viscously swipes he made.

Anger was building up in his veins.

How dare he ignore me? Make me leave! He should be grateful I didn't kill him! He should be flattered I find him attractive!

A hiss left his lips when he accidentally cuts himself. The blade ran across his thumb and slices his skin. The pain was dull from being used to pain being inflicted on. His thumb started to throb like a pulsing heart. He sticks his thumb in his mouth and started to suck the blood. His tongue runs over the cut and made him imagine what it would be like if he did this with Cody.

The thought of running his tongue over any wound of Cody's sent an excited chill up Adrian's spine. Licking away the blood from Cody's skin. Tasting him as if he was sweet candy. His body grew warm and tight at the thought.

He lets go of his thumb with a pop. Blood stained his teeth and lips. The cut still bled but not as quickly. Adrian examined the cut and saw it wasn't deep. It wouldn't need stitches.

Suddenly, his computer lit up with an alerting beep. Adrian looks at his laptop that sat on the floor.

It was a state of the art Apple laptop. He had bought it with the money he collected, using wireless connections to keep himself from being detected. He set up a fake email for new jobs. If anyone tried to hack into it, they would be given a virus.

Adrian slides off his bed with a grunt. The bruises he received from Cody were surprisingly sore. He's faced tough targets before, but somehow Cody was one of the toughest. He runs his fingers over the bruise on his throat that Cody gave him. For a moment, Adrian thought Cody might've actually killed him.

Picking up his laptop, he clicks it on as he sits back down on his bed. His screensaver was of the notorious killer, Jack the Ripper. One of the many people he admires.

The beep was an alert he put on for local murders, mostly his own. It was an update on Takanawa's murder case. Apparently, the police had arrested Takanawa's daughter Keiko for questioning. There was a picture of policemen arresting her. Adrian laughed at how disheveled she looked in the picture. It looked like she hadn't slept in days.

One way or another, they always find out, Adrian thought with a sneer. All I need to do is make sure that she doesn't confess.

Without realizing it, he starts typing in past home invasions in America. His eyes were glazed over as he read over articles from all over. Some had pictures attached and he scanned them for a familiar face. He always recognizes a face but didn't know how young Cody was when he had lost his parents.

The dates started going backwards until Adrian finally found it. The article was labeled Family of Three: Two Dead in Home Invasion. He clicks on the link and a picture popped up in the article. A tall, blond haired man and a small, brown haired woman stood side by side. Between them was a twelve-year old boy. Adrian recognized the boy immediately.

Shaggy brown hair, high cheekbones, and brown eyes. He looked about five-foot-two in the picture. Cody had a very big growth spurt.

A smile slowly grew on Adrian's face as he looked at Cody's screen face. He was just so cute. Checking the date, Adrian was surprised to see the article was dated five years ago. A few months after Adrian killed his father and finally escaped. "Cody Winters, you have such an interesting background." Adrian said out loud. The smile slowly turns to a sadistic one. No wonder you peeked my interest.

The club was pounding with lively music and people. They danced erotically to the music to attract partners. Wearing small clothes to show a lot of skin. The pulsing lights made his head slightly throb.

His drink burned his throat nicely. He didn't buy it; a girl bought it to try and peek his interest. Despite her being very attractive, Adrian found her whorish with the way she dressed. After letting her down easy, Adrian drank the drink happily.

The taste of the liquor reminded him of Cody. It gave his energy a kick and made him feel warm inside. Adrian silently wished it was Cody he was tasting.

"'Scuse me." someone said as they shoved their way to the bar next to him.

Adrian growled at the man but shakes it off. He settles into his seat, and quietly viewed the man that bumped into him. The man was a little overdressed for a club like this. He wore a grey business suit that looked a little expensive. His hair was a dark brown with some grey in it. Hate to admit it, he has good taste, Adrian thought.

The man was too busy talking on his phone to notice Adrian's watching. "Yeah . . . I found Cody and that boy was surprised seeing me." he said a little loud. Adrian froze when he heard his boy's name, but quickly shrugs it off, thinking it was just another Cody. Except he continues listening.

"That day five years ago should've ended with them all . . . don't . . . don't worry, I'll get the money. My brother should've given me that money long ago. Winters won't know what hit him." he ended his call with a laugh. He pockets his phone and orders a beer from the bartender.

The look Adrian was giving him could've killed anyone. Insanity was clearly in his eyes. His top lip curled up in a snarl, revealing his sharpened canines.

He is talking about Cody, Adrian thought. He curls his fingers around his drink and was ready to break it over the man's head. That bastard is going to kill Cody! I can't let that happen, Adrian thought.

The man stuffs his phone in his back pocket that was facing Adrian. He takes a sip of his drink and watches the dancers. Unknowingly being watched by a serial killer.

Taking in a deep breath, Adrian puts on a calm face and says,"You from around here? You sure don't look like it." His voice changed to a practiced Brooklyn accent. He leans in and sniffs the man to recognize his scent, having a good sense of smell. The man smelled of cheap cologne that re-sembled cinnamon but with sweat added to it. It was gross but would be recognizable.

His head whipped around to face Adrian. His brown eyes looked wild when he saw him. "Ever heard of minding your business?" he snapped at Adrian. It takes all Adrian had to not shank him then. "Calm down, man. I'm just wondering what a businessman like you is in a place like this?" Adrian said defensively.

"Again, ever heard of minding your own business?" he re-peated angrily. Then he stalked off through the crowd. As he walked away, Adrian slipped his hand in his back pocket and snatched his wallet. He easily stuffs it down his jeans without problem. "Whatever, man." Adrian said with a scoff, but it slowly turns to a creepy smile.

Chapter 14

C ody

"Is this for real!?" Michaela exclaimed as she stared at the piece of paper. She laid on Cody's bed and held his inheritance sheet high above her head. Her legs were extended above her head, and she starts kicking like an excited little kid. "You are loaded!" she yelled excitedly.

Despite how amusing it was seeing his best friend all excited, Cody couldn't help but be confused. He just found out he was going to inherit a million dollars. And he never even knew it. Thoughts ran through Cody's head as he tries to figure out how his father got so much money.

Savings? Inheritance from his parents? Cody thought but couldn't figure out. Gears turned in his head and it started to give him a headache. This was more confusing than him.

"I won't be getting the money till I'm eighteen so don't get too excited." Cody said as he snatches the paper from Michaela. "And your birthday is in a couple of months!" Michaela reminded him. Rolling his eyes at her, Cody couldn't stop himself from laughing. But it stopped quickly. "I still don't know if I should believe this Michael guy. For all I know this is some weirdo wanting the money my father gave me." he said.

That man's voice is also very similar to that burglar, Cody thought. Anger started to sizzle in his bones. He didn't know if Michael was one of the burglars, but he knew that he was there. That voice was so familiar. The same as the leader . . .

The first thing Cody sees is the door bursting open. The bang made him scream in fright as he drops his glass of water. Water and glass spread all over the floor. Shards of glass cut his feet but that wasn't important.

"DOWN ON THE FUCKING GROUND!" screamed the first person to burst through the door. Four more men came in after him. Guns were raised and aiming at Cody and his mother.

Cody's mother quickly pushes Cody behind her. He could feel her shaking in fear but refused to show it. "Who are you!? What are you doing?!" she demanded in a forced tone, trying to be brave. Cody peeks from behind and stares at the large man with the ski mask. He recognized the gun as the kind his dad uses.

"Get down on the ground!" the man ordered again. He was now just a few feet away from Cody's mother. The gun was so close to her face.

"Don't hurt my mom!" Cody screamed. He ran in front of his mom and stood in front of the gun. "My dad is a police officer! You'll get arrested for this!" he yelled.

Through the thick layer of black wool, the man glared at Cody with his cold eyes. He changes his aim and aims the gun at Cody's face. "Like I care." the man sneered.

Shots were fired from behind Cody. He ducks when bullets hit pictures on the wall and glass flew everywhere. "GET AWAY FROM MY FAMILY!" screamed Cody's father.

Arms wrapped around Cody, and he was carried away. He caught a glimpse of his father standing there with his gun. A strong look was on his face as he faced the intruders. Cody wished he said something as his mother quickly guided him away. Bullets flew over their head as they turned down the hallway.

Shouts from his father and the intruders echoed through the air. Cody wanted to go back to help but his mom held a tight grip on his shirt. He was led to the basement door, and his mom opened it up quietly. "Go downstairs and hide. Don't make a sound." she ordered in a hushed tone. "What about you?" Cody asked scared; he couldn't hear his father's voice anymore. "I'll be right down. Do not make a sound and do not come out till me or your father come to get you." his mother ordered before lightly pushing Cody down the basement stairs.

The door shut behind him but he doesn't turn back. He follows his mother's orders and silently runs downstairs. The creaks in the stairs were small and couldn't be heard over the gunshots. Screams from his mother sprung tears from his eyes.

Cody couldn't see anything in the basement. The smell of rotting walls and the drips of leaking water was overwhelming. He takes in a deep breath and walks to the back right corner. Pressing his back against the wall, he slowly slips down to the floor.

More gunshots were fired, and Cody heard his mother scream. He swears he heard a thump right above him. Please let that be one of the intruders, Cody thought. He hides his face in his knees and silently begs for this nightmare to end.

It only felt like moments went by when the basement door opens. Picking up his head, Cody saw a beam of light peering down the stairs. He waited to hear his father or mother but dreads that it maybe one of the intruders. Loud footsteps walked down the stairs and were followed with another pair of footsteps.

Fear shakes him to the bone as he waits. Cody couldn't blink as he prepares to see who was walking downstairs.

"Plymouth Police Department, is anyone down here?" demanded man with a strong voice. Cody didn't move, afraid that the person could be one of the intruders pretending to be a cop. He bites his bottom lip and keeps himself quiet.

Two figures stepped down from the staircase. They flashed their flashlights around the room. Cody hopes that they skim passed him but his hopes die immediately. Two flashlights shine on his curled up form. Cody grunts and hides away from the bright light.

"Are you Cody Winters?" asked the same man with the strong voice.

Picking up his head, Cody stares up at two real police officers. They were both well built but aged to their middle years. "Yes?" Cody said unsurely.

The cops exchange looks before the cop on the left got on his knees and holds his hand out to Cody. "I'm sorry, son. But your parents are gone." he said solemnly.

"Cody?"

Michaela's voice woke him from his daze. He blinks away the memory and saw she was looking at him in worry. "Sorry. Just spaced out." Cody said; straightening up his posture.

He could tell she didn't believe him because she gives him that look. "Don't give me the Look!" Cody whined like a little kid. "Oh I'll keep giving you the look till you tell me what you are hiding!" Michaela said as she literally pounces on him. Her weight knocked him backwards, and the chair gave out from under them.

Both letting out yelps, Michaela and Cody tumble to the floor. It knocked the breath out of the both of them.

"I thought I told you that this chair can be slippery." Cody groaned. He was having trouble breathing because Michaela was on his chest. "I forgot." Michaela said with a grunt. She pushes herself up with her arms but doesn't get up right away.

The two realize how close they were to one another. Their eyes connect and stood still. Cody could feel her nose brush his own. He could smell her scent that consisted of jasmine and a hint of banana.

Slowly, Michaela leans in till their lips were just inches away. Her breath danced on his lips. "M-Michaela," he stuttered.

"Well ain't this something?" spoke that cursed voice of Adrian.

Michaela and Cody turn their heads to the window. They discover Adrian sitting on the windowsill with a knife in his hand. He looked both amused and irked at the sight that was in front of him.

"Fuck my life." Cody said.

Chapter 15

A drian

Jealousy and anger bubbled in his veins at the sight before him. Utter revulsion was in his eyes though he kept a straight face. His lip curled upward in a snarl.

He risked his life by returning to the neighborhood, climbing up the side of Cody's house to deliver the news of his next target's ambitions. Only to find his boy being straddled by some harlot.

They didn't notice him at the window or when he slipped in. They were too busy staring into each other's eyes. (Ugh.) Their lips were so close to touching that he had to stop them immediately.

"Well ain't this something?" he said darkly, situating himself on the windowsill. His knife was held tightly in his hand that could be viewed by the two.

Cody and the bitch turned their heads and saw Adrian sitting there. Horror was in Cody's eyes while confusion yet fear was in the girl's. You should be afraid, bitch, Adrian thought. He smiles at the two as if they were old friends. "I come to deliver some news, Winters. But I guess your occupied." The last word was spoken bitterly.

Quickly, Cody and the girl got up and brush themselves off. Adrian wanted to shove the two away but kept still. He wasn't here to kill anyone.

Yet . . .

"What the hell are you doing here? I told you I would call the cops if you came anywhere near this place!" Cody snapped vivaciously. Anger was clear on his face. But it soon changed when he realizes something. "How do you know my last name?" he demanded quite frightened.

The girl exchanges glances at Adrian and Cody. She tried to tell what was going on, clearly not knowing who Adrian was.

"How I know is not why I'm here. I'm here because you have a target on your head." Adrian said as he takes out the wallet he stole. He jumps off the sill and steps toward Cody.

Noticing the tension in his bones and stillness in his stance, Adrian steps back a step. "Do you know this man?" he asked as he flips open the wallet. He went through the man's wallet. (And may have stolen the three hundred dollars inside.) There wasn't anything specific that he could find without looking the guy up. But he was busy hurrying to Cody to look.

Cody looked at the wallet and realization appeared on his face. He snatches the wallet from Adrian's grasp and views it closer. "Where did you get this?" he demanded incredulously. "This man was talking on the phone about you. Said something about 'he's going to get it' and 'his brother should've given me the money'." Adrian puts air quotes on what the man said.

"Is he talking about your uncle?" the girl asked. To be honest, Adrian forgot she was there. "I think he is." Cody said. He stares at the ID of the man with distaste. "I knew he was no good." he said angrily.

"Back up a second. This man is your uncle?" Adrian asked, snatching the wallet back to view the man's face on the ID. "And I thought my life was messed up." he said once he notices the resemblance in the picture and Cody. Then he tosses it back to Cody. "So I have to kill your uncle? That'll be something." Adrian said casually.

"Kill?!" Michaela said in a squeaky voice. Her voice made Adrian cringe. "God, what are you? A mouse?" he asked annoyed. "Stop it, Adrian. I'm thankful for you informing me about Michael, but now I want you to leave." Cody ordered. He starts to go through the wallet with a sour look. Boy, did Adrian wish to change the look on Cody's face. (Hopefully into a pleasure-filled one.)

Frowning, Adrian says,"I'm here to protect you. I ain't leaving." He crosses his arms and cocks out his hip like a girl. Cody looked about ready to explode as he gave Adrian the stink eye.

"Can someone tell me what is going on?!" Michaela all but screamed. She pointed at Adrian and shouts,"Who is he?" Dear God, someone shut this girl up, Adrian thought. "No one important, Michaela," Cody told her quickly. He spins Adrian around and starts pushing him toward the window. "He's just about to leave." Cody finished with a shove to Adrian's back.

No one important?! Adrian thought incredulously. "Now wait a second," he started as he turned around. "I have every right to be here as much as this girl. I'm here to keep you safe from that uncle of yours." he finished, crossing his arms. "There are such things as police!" Cody exclaimed with a wave of his arms. "My way is easier!" Adrian snapped back.

Suddenly, the two were smacked in the forehead. Their heads rung like a bell. They turn to face Michaela, and she had her hands on her hips and a glare that even scared Adrian. "Both of you are bickering like an old married couple. Now," she looks at Cody. "Cody, if you don't tell me who he is, I'm gonna march downstairs and tell Sarah that a man just broke into your home and about Michael." she finished with a hard look.

Sharing a look, Adrian and Cody look back at Michaela. And back at each other.

"Well . . . he's sorta . . . " Cody began awkwardly.

"We're lovers." Adrian stated.

Two heads snapped toward Adrian. One pair of eyes showed disbelief while the other was horrified. "WE ARE NOT LOVERS!" Cody screamed. "Not yet." Adrian mumbled. "Someone start telling me the truth or I'll start breaking heads!" Michaela threatened angrily.

"He's the man that killed Takanawa!" Cody just blurted out.

Immediately, everything went quiet. Michaela's eyes widened in horror and looked at Adrian in fear. She went rigid, and Adrian could practically hear her heart pounding. "Aren't you subtle?" Adrian commented toward Cody with a smirk. "Shut it." Cody snapped.

"Y-You killed Takanawa . . . " Michaela stuttered. "Just as Cody said," Adrian said. "Don't worry, I'm not here to kill you or him. Just came to warn him." he finished with a creepy smile. He leans in and says,"I'm here to protect Cody because he's mine."

Michaela backed away till she touched the wall. "Michaela, he was hired to kill him by Takanawa's daughter. And he won't hurt you." Cody assured her. He reached out to her but she smacks his hand away. "You've been talking to a murderer! Are you friends with him?" she asked horrified. "No! He tried to kill me last night!" Cody yelled. "That was before I took a liking to you!" Adrian piped up. "Again! Shut up!" Cody shouted.

Quickly, Michaela shoves Cody away and runs out of his room. "Michaela, wait!" Cody shouted as he ran after her. "Son of a bitch." Adrian said as he ran after them. Nearly tripping over the iguana when he entered the hallway. He jumped on one foot and regained his footing. "Weird-ass lizard!" Adrian cried.

"Sarah! Sarah, where are you?" Michaela screamed as she ran downstairs. "She's not home! She's still at work! Please stop and let me explain!" Cody begged as he slid down the rail to catch up to Michaela. He was able to reach her and grabs her by the shoulders. "Don't touch me!" she screamed and smacked Cody across the face.

Anger unfolded inside of Adrian as he let out a roar. He practically flew down the stairs and attacked Michaela. Her body hit the wall and everything shook. Adrian clamped his left hand on her throat as the other took out his knife. "Lay a hand on him again and I'll slit your throat." Adrian threatened coldly. "No you won't!" Cody yelled and shoved Adrian away. "You're not killing anyone!"

Growling viscously, Adrian was about to reprimand him but saw Cody held Adrian's knife. Those brown eyes held ice that froze Adrian down to the core. "Put down the knife, Cody." Adrian demanded softly. After witnessing Cody's strength, Adrian knew that Cody can take him on. "If you kill Michaela, I will kill you." Cody growled. The two were quiet as they glared at each other.

"Cody . . . " Michaela spoke up.

Cody looks at Michaela, and she was looking at him with a different look. "I won't tell anyone about him," she points at Adrian. "But I'm telling the police about Michael." she finished seriously. She brushes passed Cody and heads to the door. "Michaela, wait!" Cody said.

"Stop." Adrian said, his voice loud and reverberating. Michaela froze mid-step and looked back at Adrian. "You're not telling anyone about Cody's uncle. I'm gonna take care of him myself." Adrian said. He steps up to Michaela and looks at her directly in the eye. "Trust me on this. The police can't be involved." he said. "And why not?" Michaela asked coldly.

"He killed Cody's parents." Adrian stated.

Horror reached her face. "For the money." she said suddenly. She looked at Cody with realization. "Michael is after the money." she said.

"Money? What money?" Adrian asked confused. "Cody was given his father's will today. He has inherited a million dollars." Michaela said.

Chapter 16

Cody

His eyes were wide open and there was no feeling of sleep. He tried to fall asleep but the recent events were plaguing his mind.

Just two hours ago, Michaela meets Adrian under bad circumstances. She tries to flee and tell the police. He and Adrian were able to convince her not to with some encouraging. (By that, I mean by Adrian threatening her.) Now she is not going to expose Adrian, but Cody didn't know how long that will last.

After that awkward moment, Michaela heads home while Adrian remained. Though not by Cody's choosing.

"You know you can leave, right?" Cody asked, cutting the silence in his bedroom. "There is no need for you to stay." he said rather annoyed. "Im keeping an eye on you. Who knows when Michael will strike." Adrian said from his spot on the floor. Groaning, Cody rolls onto his side to flip the switch to his bedside lamp. Light flooded only half the room but revealed Adrian lying on the ground. He laying on a inflatable mattress Sarah kept around. Izzy was curled up beside him and was passed asleep.

"And how am I suppose to explain to Sarah why there is a twenty-something-year old man in my bedroom?" Cody asked.

Adrian laughed. "I'll be gone before you wake up. Im not that reckless." he said gloatingly. Earning him a whack to the head with a pillow that was thrown at him. "You are that reckless." Cody denied Adrian. He switches off the light and lays back down on his back. Taking in a deep breath, Cody slowly began to fall asleep. His heart was finally starting to calm down.

Just as he was close to falling asleep, something slips into the bed beside him. Cody's eyes shot open as an arm lays itself across his chest. He looks down at the arm then at the owner. Adrian was settling into his sleep, looking as if what he was doing is completely normal.

"What the hell are you doing?" Cody asked annoyed. Adrian's face was so close to his own that he could feel the killer's breath against his face. He stared at the older male's face, looking over every pore and crevice. The scar on Adrian's eyebrow seemed to glow from so close. He hated to admit it, but Adrian was gorgeous.

"I can't sleep on that mattress, and I want to keep a careful eye on you." Adrian said as he literally nuzzles against the back of Cody's neck. Cody's neck seized up as he felt Adrian's lips graze his skin. "Well I need fucking space." Cody hissed as he shuffles a few inches away from Adrian. The grip on his waist tightened and Cody was pulled into Adrian's bare chest. "Where is your shirt?" Cody asked with a squeak. "I sleep in my underwear." Adrian replied with a low chuckle. Then he emphasizes his point by tangling one of his bare legs with Cody's clothed ones.

Cody's heart felt like it was about to leap out of his chest when he felt the rumble of Adrian's chuckle. His skin started to grow warmer and warmer. "Don't try anything funny." Cody growled as he tried to keep himself under control. The arm resting on his stomach curled around his waist. He felt the bed move and could sense Adrian hovering over him.

Cody looks up at Adrian and their noses brush against each other. His breath got caught in his throat as Cody stared into those ice blue eyes. "Will this be funny?" Adrian asked in a whisper. Then he leans in and kisses Cody fully on the lips.

The taste of Adrian's lips sent a pleasurable chill up Cody's spine. But he didn't want it. Cody tries to pull away, but Adrian's grip tightened to a bone-crushing one. Adrian presses his lips harder against Cody's till it hurt. He could feel Adrian's teeth as the kiss continued. Heat flooded his face and flows down to his toes.

"Just accept it." Adrian whispered in between their lips.

Slowly, Cody's body started to respond to Adrian's kiss. He turns his body to face Adrian and began to return the kiss. Adrian's lips began to rumble in a growl as he slips his tongue into Cody's mouth without any resistance. His arms slip around Cody's waist, and he pulls Cody up on to his chest.

Quickly breaking away to breathe, Cody and Adrian stare at each other's eyes. Cody's face felt flushed from lack of air while Adrian had a big shit-eating smile on his face. "I knew you'd fall for me." Adrian gloated. A snarl curled up on

Cody's lips. "Just shut up and kiss me." Cody snapped before swooping down and kissing Adrian again.

He couldn't believe what he was doing. His first kiss was not only with a man but with a serial killer. But he couldn't care less now. It felt like his mind just shut down as he kissed Adrian. He runs his fingers through his hair and raked his nails down his scalp.

Adrian rests his hands on Cody's hips and gave them a squeeze. His nails sank into Cody's skin but it tickled more than hurt. The possessiveness in his grip exhilarated Cody. He squeezes his legs against Adrian's waist and let out a growl of his own. "Becoming animal, are we?" Adrian joked with a smirk.

There was an unknown sensation bubbling up inside of Cody, slowly breaching the surface of his skin. He presses his forehead against Adrian's chest and says,"You're not the only one with a monster inside." Untangling his fingers from Adrian's hair, he sinks his nails into Adrian's shoulders. His body shook in what he didn't know was fear or excitement. "W-What is this feeling?" Cody asked in a shaky tone.

"Warmth in your stomach? Shaking to the core?" Adrian asked, listing off the sensations Cody was feeling. "It's called lust," he whispered in Cody's ear. "It's different for everyone else." he finished with a soft bite on Cody's earlobe. "Mine comes with the feel of pain." Adrian said before beginning to run his lips down Cody's throat.

A fire was raging in the pit of Cody's stomach. His mouth opened wide as he let out soft moans. This feeling was so foreign to him; and he loved it.

Suddenly, the familiar sound of a door opening and closing echoed faintly through the house. Adrian's mouth froze in mid-nip. Cody froze completely as he looks at his door. "Sarah's home." he stared. "You don't know that. It could be a burglar or Michael." Adrian said as he tries to continue his bites. "Yet you're still fucking kissing me?" Cody hissed as he shoves Adrian away before climbing off the bed.

A defeated whine escaped Adrian as he remained on the bed watching as Cody grabs a bat that hung on the wall. "I like the risk." Adrian said. That gave Cody a lucid thought at what Adrian meant. He shuddered at that and shakes his head to rid the thought. "Just keep quiet. If it is Sarah, I'm not gonna explain why you're here." Cody said annoyed. "Aw baby," Adrian whined. It took all of Cody had not to just bash Adrian's head in.

Stepping out of his bedroom, Cody peers around the corner. His heart was hammering against his chest as he thought of who could be in the house. He sees a light at the bottom of the staircase. No burglar or even Michael would turn on the light. It had to be Sarah.

"Sarah? Is that you?" Cody called out.

"Yeah, it's me!" Sarah called back.

A sigh of relief was let out as Cody lowers the bat. "I'm heading back to bed. There's some left over lasagna if you want any." Cody said. "Already cooking! Night!" Sarah shouted. "Night!" Cody shouted back. He turns back to his bedroom but stopped. His mind replayed what he had just done. 'I made out with a damn killer,' he thought incredulously. 'I'm gonna need to kick him out,' he thought with some dread. For some reason, his heart dropped at the idea of getting rid of Adrian.

Quickly shaking away his thoughts, Cody returns to his room, preparing for a fight. Only, he is greeted with an empty room besides Izzy.

There were no signs of Adrian. His clothes weren't on the floor, no sign of his knife. Cody checked the closet to make sure he wasn't hiding in there again.

Nope. Not there.

'Where the hell did you go?' Cody thought in confusion. He sets his bat down on the desk before returning to his bed. When he hopped on his bed, he feels a crinkle noise under him. Cody reaches underneath and snatches a folded piece of paper. He unfolds it buy couldn't read because of the darkness.

Flipping on the light, much to the displeasure of Izzy, Cody reads the note.

Decided to head home. Why don't we continue after our date tomorrow?

Adrian

After rereading the note, Cody went from confused to frantic. 'WHAT DATE?!' he thought in horror.

Chapter 17

A drian

"Here's your iced coffee," said the barista. She hands him a medium sized cup with a flirtatious wink. Her eyebrow ring gleamed in the shop's light at her wink. Adrian just wanted to rip it off and shove it down her throat.

Adrian only smiles at her and pays with a ten dollar bill, giving her the change as a tip. (And hoping she wouldn't try to flirt with him again.) "Anything else?" she asked. (Guess not.) "Im fine. Thank you." Adrian said with a small wave. He walks away from the counter and sits down at a booth that viewed the street. Thankful that she doesn't try to get his attention.

Instead of looking out the window or drinking his coffee, Adrian looks in front of him. Two booths ahead of him was his target. Michael Winters.

Adrian woke up that morning with a goal. To scope out Michael and watch for any weaknesses. He knew that he had to take notes on Michael. Over the years, Adrian learned to study his targets. After a few mistakes in the past, he made sure to keep tabs on them.

Currently, Michael was chatting on the phone. An annoyed look was on his ugly face. Probably noticed his wallet was missing. Wonder how long it took him to notice, Adrian mused with a smirk.

Adrian takes a sip of his coffee and starts taking notes on his small notepad. His eyes gave off a psychotic glint as he views Michael. Watching him as a hawk would view prey.

Jotting down a few notes, he takes notice of how Michael handled himself. His dominate hand was his right from the way he held his phone and his hair was thinning but not from age. Adrian notices Michael's thin skin and the bags around his eyes from where he sat. 'He's ill', Adrian thought in realization.

He quickly scribbles his thoughts down on the paper. Adrian glances up again and saw Michael was no longer there. 'Shit,' he thought as he viewed the coffee shop. His pulse quickened as he worried that Michael left.

His eyes quickly find Michael just at the entrance. The man exited the coffee shop in a brisk pace. Adrian cursed under his breath as he hastily collects his things and chases after Michael. He tosses his coffee in the trash as he left with a flick of his wrist as he left the shop.

Adrian hurried after Michael but kept equal distance from him. He throws his hoodie over his head and had his eyes downcast. About twenty feet away from Michael, he kept his eyes at the man's feet. Watching closely so he wouldn't lose sight of Michael.

Instincts kicked in and he tunes in his ears, closing out all of the noises and focusing on Michael. He could faintly hear Michael talking on his phone. 'God, how long does he talk on that phone?' Adrian thought.

The wind blew south and drifted toward Adrian. His ears twitched as he listened closely.

"I'll find . . . I called the company to . . . I'll find that . . ." Michael's voice faded in and out. It irked Adrian that he couldn't hear enough. So he takes his chances and speeds up his walk toward Michael. His eyes were locked on the back of Michael's head. Adrian imagined that he was bashing his skull in with his own hands.

He was close enough to be just a few feet behind Michael. Not close enough to notice but enough to hear Michael clearly.

"That kid is like his father, not smart at all. I'll get him when he least expects it." Michael spoke into his phone. A growl rumbled in Adrian's throat. 'That bastard,' Adrian thought angrily. He reaches into his jacket pocket to grab the small icepick he handcrafted. His anger was building up over the edge.

Just seconds before committing another murder, Adrian changes his mind and lets go of the icepick. He couldn't expose himself yet. That man will know who Adrian is soon enough.

He stops walking and lets Michael walk away. That man unknowing that he was nearly murdered just then.

The walk back to his apartment never felt so painful. Adrian wanted to turn back around and finish off Michael then and there. But he fought his killer instincts. He knew that Michael wasn't his kill. It was Cody's.

He takes the elevator instead of the stairs. His breath was raspy and his chest hurt. Never has he felt pain from choosing not to kill a person. He is usually calm when he holds back but not this time.

The elevator stopped two floors below his floor. A mother and son stepped inside. Adrian pressed himself against the wall to give them room. The mother pushed the lobby button and waited quietly.

Luckily, the elevator took them to his floor first. He stepped out with a small smile to the mother and son. His mind gave him the painful reminder of his mother and him. When the elevator doors shut, he let out a growl. Adrian used to hope that his mother would return to patch up the wounds in his father and Adrian. That hope ended when his father started hitting him with a belt.

Adrian entered his apartment with a big sigh. A headache was growing that was worse than Cody's attacks. He throws off his jacket and shirt, feeling his skin become hot. Sweat glistened his pale skin and tattoos.

'Did I catch Cody's sickness?' Adrian thought as he wipes away sweat from his forehead.

Suddenly, there was a knock at the door. Adrian tenses up as he looks at the door. "NYPD, open the door." shouted a man on the other side.

'Shit,' Adrian thought as he quickly puts on his shirt and hides the icepick by stuffing it in a drawer. "Coming," he said as he finishes looking over the living room, making sure to not have any evidence. Once he's sure everything is hidden, Adrian heads to the door.

He opens the door and is greeted by two men in business suits. One was smaller than the other. The smaller one had a buzzcut with black hair and bushy eyebrows. The bigger man had shaggy brown hair and there was a scar on his eyebrow. Adrian recognized them as the leading officers in Takanawa's murder case.

"May I help you officers?" Adrian asked with feigned innocence.

"Jonathan Brice?" asked the big guy.

"That's me." Adrian said, recognizing his alias name. "I'm Detective Jackson and this is Detective Johns. We are homicide detectives looking into the murder of Yuuta Takanawa." said the big officer. 'Bitch must've squealed,' Adrian thought angrily. "Im sorry but I don't know a Yuuta Takanawa. I moved to New York not too long ago." he said, half lying-half speaking the truth.

Detective Johns stepped up and takes out a picture. He shows the picture to Adrian, and he sees that it was a picture of Keiko. "Do you know this girl?" Detective Johns asked.

Pretending to take a look of the picture, Adrian shakes his head. "I don't know her personally but I think I've seen her on the news," he said half-truthfully. "Is there anything else you need to ask? I have a date to prepare for." Adrian said with a smile.

A sigh escaped from Detective Jackson. "Listen, Keiko Takanawa told us she talked to a man with your description. Did you speak with Keiko?" he demanded coldly. He gave Adrian a hard glare that was daring Adrian to lie. "No, I have not, Officer." he drawled out 'officer' in a taunting tone.

"Well then, since you're a person of interest in the murder case, we advise you not to leave town. We may have follow up questions for you." Detective Johns said as he literally pulls Jackson away from the doorway. "Yes, Sir," Adrian said with a smile before shutting the door. The second he closes the door, the smile disappeared from his face.

"Fuck."

Chapter 18

C ody

His foot tapped rapidly as he tries to focus on the test. Staring down at the question as if it was on fire. He was on the final question and now he was in a stump. With five minutes left of class, he had to be quick but also not rush.

'Don't freak out now,' Cody begged to himself silently.

The question never looked so far away. Cody cursed under his breath as he taps the tip of his pencil against his desk. All his mind was focusing on was the note Adrian left him. He refused to believe it was a real date. But with Adrian, who knows what it really means. That man's mood changes quicker than Izzy can slap your ankles.

Cody didn't have a wink of sleep because his thoughts were latched onto Adrian. He was surprised he actually got out of bed.

Something suddenly taps Cody on the shoulder. He turns his head to look at his desk neighbor. His look became sour when he saw it was his bully, Jack Baron. A jock on the football team and was somehow on the student council. (Cody's guess was he rigged the vote.)

The first day Cody came to this school, Jack has made it his goal to make Cody's life miserable.

"What do you want, Jack?" Cody hissed. His eyes narrowed at the big jock in distaste. Unlike the other nobodies, he wasn't afraid of his bullies. "Can you give me the answer for one through fifteen?" Jack asked with a sneer. "That's all the damn questions!" Cody all but shouted.

The final bell rung and Cody never felt so relieved. Looking back at his test, he guesses on the final question and turns it in.

When he attempts to leave the classroom, he was grabbed by his backpack. Cody yelped as he stumbled back. Luckily, he was able to catch himself from falling. He fixes his stance and looks at who grabbed him, having an idea who it was.

And he was right.

Jack stood there smirking with one of his goons standing beside him. "What do you want now?" Cody demanded angrily. Inside, he was confused, he didn't know where this confidence was coming from. Despite not being afraid of bullies, he tries to stay under their radar. This was new to him.

"You've been avoiding me, Winters. Im failing science and I need your notes. So just hand them over and I'll give 'em back." Jack said, obviously lying to Cody's face. Cody just wanted to punch Jack in the face. Just imagining that made him smile evilly. "Like hell I'll give them to you," Cody simple stated before leaving he classroom, giving Jack the bird.

'Adrian is getting into my head. I'm actually acting like him.' Cody thought.

Students still filled the hallways as they hurried to their cars or buses. Cody was careful to slip through the swarming bodies to escape Jack and his goons. He spares a glance behind him and saw Jack was pursuing him. That cocky smile was replaced with a determined look. It made Cody realize he may get a beating.

'Shit,' Cody thought as he takes a different route instead of going to the bus loop. He takes the east hallway that lead to the front entrance of the school. His walk sped up to a run. Then to a sprint.

He bursted through the doors and ran down the walkway.

"Get back here, Winters!"

Adrenaline pumped through Cody's veins. It was the same as the time when he attacked Adrian. "Come and get me!" he yelled tauntingly. He actually started to laugh like a madman.

He ran off the school grounds and ran across a busy street. People honked their horns at Cody but he kept on running. He doesn't know whether Jack followed but didn't spare a glance. Cody runs through random alleyways to try and confuse anyone who was following him.

Suddenly, he was grabbed by his hair. His neck made a snap as his head was yanked backwards. Cody cried out as he fell on the ground flat on his back. "Son of a bitch." he cursed. He opened his eyes and looked up at who grabbed him.

The upside down version of Jack never looked so threatening. "You shouldn't have fled, Winters." Jack said angrily.

A growl rumbled lowly in Cody's chest as he stands back up. Wiping away dust from his jacket, he straightens his back and glares at Jack. "I don't care what you want. I'm not your damn slave." Cody growled. He unconsciously curls his fists till he felt his knuckles pop.

Unknown anger was building up inside of Cody as he glared at Jack. "I suggest that you leave, Jack. I already have enough on my plate." Cody said. "Like I care." Jack sneered. Jack takes something out of his jersey and reveals it to be a knife.

"Jack, why do you have a knife?" Cody asked cautiously. He steps back, eyeing the knife. "I thought a good scare tactic will be good for you. I don't like people being brave with me." Jack said with a sadistic look.

'Great, another psychopath,' Cody thought. "I've already had a knife to my neck. Literally." he said with no emotion. He crosses his arms and glares at Jack. "If you think you can actually scare me, just try me." Cody sneered. He held up his arms in a way of convincing Jack.

Jack looked slightly perturbed but shook it off. He ran at Cody with the knife raised. Seeming to be content on actually killing him. Cody prepared for the attack.

At the last second, Jack stopped in his tracks as if he was shot. His legs began to wobble till he collapsed. Cody walked up to Jack with caution. "Jack?" Cody asked worriedly.

Sluggishly, Jack started to move. He reaches behind his back and seemed to grab something. Jack let out a scream as he pries something out of his back.

Horror appeared on Cody's face when he saw it was a knife. The entire blade was caked in Jack's blood. "Holy shit!" he cried out. Quickly, Cody ran over to Jack to help him. Not noticing the familiar figure in front of him.

"Why are you helping him?" asked Adrian, who Cody now just noticed.

"Did you do this?!" Cody demanded angrily. "If I didn't, he would've killed you." Adrian replied. "He was just trying to scare me! If he actually did, I would've escaped!" Cody yelled.

A frown appeared on Adrian'a face. "I know a killer when I see one. He was going to kill you." he insisted. He stepped up toward Cody, but Cody quickly grabs the knife from Jack's hand and holds it up. "Don't come any closer!" Cody ordered. His hand began to shake as he aimed the tip at Adrian.

Adrian stopped a few feet from Jack's bleeding form. "I was protecting you," he stated. "I didn't want you to get hurt."

"By killing one of my damn classmates?! If he dies, I'm held as a suspect! They'll frame me for his murder!" Cody had to keep his voice down from flat out screaming. He gets down on his knees and checks Jack's pulse. It was weak but consistent. "I'm taking him to the hospital, and you are not following me!" Cody snarled.

Using all of his strength. Cody picks up Jack and holds him in his arms like a bride. He walks passed Adrian but stops when he was right beside him. "I won't tell the police that you did it. Take it as a thank you for 'protecting me'." Cody growled before running out of the alley.

Chapter 19

Michael

For once, New York was quiet at night. The city lights looked beautiful from his wide window. It was a sight to behold.

He lit up his lighter with a flick of his thumb. Then waves the flame over the cigar hanging off his mouth.

The familiar smell of smoke wafted into his lungs as his cigar lit up. Michael flicks his lighter to get rid of the fame. He sets it down on his dresser before turning back to his bed.

An older yet younger woman slept on the left side of the bed. Completely naked. Her hair was strewn all over the pillow and seemed to create a halo effect. Bite marks and bruises covered her skin from Michael's doing. Her large breasts were slick with sweat and other juices he didn't know.

Her wet scent could be smelt from where Michael stood. The smell made him shiver excitedly. Michael walks up to the bed and crawls on top of it. The cigarette hung in between his teeth as he continued breathing it in. Smoke billowed out of his mouth as he sucked in the smoke.

Hovering over the sleeping woman, he slowly lays down beside her. He wraps his arms around her thin, tattooed waist. His hands began to roam over her chest. Lightly caressing her soft mounds.

She moaned softly in her sleep. Goosebumps ran up her body in a wave. Michael smirked at how easy she's aroused. He continues to caress her skin till she squirmed.

'So easily entertained,' he thought, 'I wonder if Cody will be just easy.'

Chapter 20

C ody

He wishes he wasn't used to the sound of the hospital. All of the hustling of feet and the beeps of an EKG. His heart started to weigh ton after ton. It was because of him that Jack was in this mess. (Of course, if Jack didn't chase after him, he might've not been stabbed.)

Cody ran two blocks to get to the hospital. He didn't slow down nor let anyone get in his way. No way was he letting someone else die with him doing nothing.

Nurses flooded all around him once they caught sight of Jack in his arms. They screamed for doctors and to prepare for surgery. None of them were strong enough to carry Jack so they guided Cody to a gurney to place him before they wheeled Jack away.

It was two hours ago, yet it still felt like it just happened. Doctors checked Cody for any injuries. They asked questions about how Jack got stabbed. He half-lied, saying that Jack was just trying to scare him and during the fear Cody was feeling, he didn't catch sight of the stabber. All he said was that his best guess was that the attacker threw the knife to avoid being seen.

The hospital said he could leave but he refused. It was his fault Jack was in this mess. He wanted to stay till he knew Jack was alright.

A doctor with blood stained on his shirt came to him about an hour after they wheeled Jack off. He explained to Cody that Jack survived the operation. That the knife didn't sever any important arteries or organs. But he could've died from blood loss if Cody didn't get to the hospital in time.

Cody was relieved to hear the news but still stayed. He wanted to see Jack when he was awake. It made him realize that he should've called Sarah awhile ago.

"WHERE IS MY SON?!" screamed a booming voice.

That man who yelled, Cody knew him all too well. He looks up to see Principle Baron storming down the hallway with his wife by his side. A male nurse was running after them, trying to keep up. "I want to know who did this to my son!" Principle Baron screamed. He didn't notice Cody as he ran passed him.

The doctor who operated on Jack stepped out of the hospital room. Luckily, he changed shirts.

"You're the kid's father, I'm guessing?" said the doctor.

"Hell, yes, I am! What the hell happened?!" demanded Principle Baron. He got in the doctor's face, his own bright red.

"Talk to Mr. Winters. He was the one who witnessed it." the doctor said as he gestured toward Cody. Principle Baron's eyes cut toward Cody, and Cody has never felt so scared. (Not even Adrian could scare him compared to Principle Baron.) "Cody Winters? One of my students?" Principle Baron questioned.

His wife, Shannon, stepped up toward Cody and gets down on one knee to be at eye-level with Cody since he was sitting down. She was a charming woman with luscious red hair and bright green eyes. Compared to Principle Baron's tall stature and balding head, Cody didn't know how they got together. "Cody, what happened? Who did this to my son?" she asked tearfully.

'Lie or truth?' Cody contemplated in his mind. He stared into her eyes and could see she was tearing up. "I didn't see who it was. The knife was thrown and I was distracted." he lied in a shaky voice. "Why were you distracted?" Shannon asked in a commanding voice. "J-Jack. He . . . was trying to scare me with a knife." Cody admitted painfully.

Horror appeared in Shannon's eyes. "LIES!" Principle Baron bellowed. "My son would never–"

"It's the truth, sir! Your son has bullied me and threatened me with a knife! But even if he did, I don't want him dead!" Cody screamed at his principle with confidence. Then he stood up and ran out of the hallway. Ignoring all the stares and Principle Baron's screaming for him to come back.

He reached the elevator and was glad to see it was just opening. A couple stepped out and headed toward the direction Cody came from. Quickly stepping into the rectangular box, Cody immediately started to rapidly tap the lobby button. He was silently begging that Principle Baron nor Shannon would come in at that second. The doors made a ding as they started to close.

Just as they were about to close, a hand shot out in between them. Cody's breath was cut short as the doors open, preparing for who was entering.

A woman about Cody's height stepped in. She wore a grey business pantsuit and had her hair up in a ponytail. "Sorry." she said in a small voice. They clashed eyes for a brief moment before she looks downcast. "It's okay." Cody said as the doors finally shut.

They were on the eleventh floor; and they waited quietly for it to end.

Cody checks his phone to see if he had any messages. Three messages from Michaela. Five from Sarah. Twenty from an unknown number. But with what the messages consisted of, Cody had a good guess who they were from.

'How the fuck did that fucker get my number!?' Cody thought.

Suddenly, heavy pressure pressed into his neck. Pain shot through his brain as he collapses. 'What the fuck?' he thought as he looked up at the only person that was in the elevator. The woman held a small injector the size of a 38 revolver. "Sorry." she repeated. Then his vision went black.

Chapter 21

A drian

'Where the hell is he?!' Adrian thought as he waited in Cody's room. He was beginning to become impatient after waiting for hours. Who stays at the hospital for three hours?

Adrian was sitting up on Cody's bed, going through his phone. There were no responses to any of his thirty text messages. But he could see they were read. "You know you can't ignore me." he said as if he was talking to Cody himself. 'I saved his ass and he repays me by screaming at me.'

The look in Cody's eyes showed hostility and fear. He threatened Adrian with the knife that the kid was using. The knife was a plain kitchen utensil, not at all threatening. (In Adrian's case that is.) Then Cody picked up the bastard and took off. Sometimes, Adrian wonders if Cody is as insane as he is.

The door to Cody's room suddenly opened, and Adrian expects the foster mother or Cody to come in. But it was actually the lizard. It scuttled over to the bed and hopped on without a sound. With only a glance at Adrian, it curls in a ball and seems to have fallen asleep.

"Some iguana." Adrian mumbles as he starts tapping on his phone. Absentmindedly rubbing his ankles where the iguana whacked him.

He uses a few hack codes that he took from one of his kills and uses it to hack into Cody's phone. (Who would've known taking a hacker's own hacks would come in handy.)

It only took a few taps until he was logged in. Adrian hacks into Cody's front camera and waits for what he sees. The image started out blurry, it was moving. He couldn't catch Cody's face or anyone else's. 'What the hell?' Adrian thought. He tries to somehow clear the imaging but he had no clue how.

"Hurry up with him! We can't have anyone see us!" suddenly spoke a woman's voice. The phone was lifted to the person's face, and it was a young woman. She looked about Adrian's age with long brown hair. Her eyes were an irregular amber color and she was covered heavily with makeup. "This dumbass's phone is locked up tight. We might need one of Michael's tech guys at his company to unlock it." she said as she seemed to try and open Cody's phone.

'Michael . . . took . . . Cody . . .' Adrian thought slowly. He stared at the woman's face, memorizing her as his next target. 'That son of a bitch is gonna kill him!' Growling viscously, he types in a text, 'I see you, bitch.' He sends it, still watching the woman's face.

The woman's face became filled with confusion but also horror. She stared at the screen, obviously reading the text. "What the hell?" she whispered. Smirking, Adrian texts again, 'You harm him. You die. I'm coming after you.'

After sending that text, Adrian stood up and exits through the window. 'First, I need some reinforcements.'

Michaela

The loud screams from the actress in the movie were so fake, but she couldn't get enough of it. It was amusing watching a defenseless girl scream. The actress ran through the house to escape the killer.

"Don't go in there! It's a trap!" Michaela screamed at the tv. She tosses some popcorn at it in the process. Once the small pieces hit the ground, her giant pit bull, Marcella ate them up.

"Good thing I didn't add butter," Michaela said with a mouthful as she watched her pet gobble the popcorn up. It was like watching a paper shredder in action. Except the bin is a stomach. And the food will make her gassy. (Never fun for her.)

"Good thing your parents aren't home." someone spoke up from behind her.

"AHHHHH!" Michaela screamed at the top of her lungs as she throws the giant bowl of popcorn into the air. She tosses herself off the couch and spun around ungracefully to see who snuck up on her. Her weapon . . . a remote.

Adrian stood there dressed all in black with his hoodie over his fiery red hair. He had his hands stuffed in his pockets and looked at ease. When he saw Michaela's weapon, he quirked an eyebrow. "So threatening," he taunted. "I wonder if I'll survive." he finished with a smirk.

"What are YOU doing here?!" Michaela demanded angrily but also frightened. Her hands started to shake as they held the remote. "Not here to kill you, that's for sure." Adrian guaranteed.

Marcella walked up to Adrian in curiousness. She didn't seem to sense any threat because she sat down and pawed his leg. "Traitor." Michaela growled. Adrian laughed and began to scratch Marcella's head. "Not my fault animals love me." Adrian bragged. "Now lets get down to business." he said suddenly.

"What business?" Michaela demanded.

"Cody was kidnapped just hours ago," Adrian responded in distaste. "Michael took him."

"What!" Michaela screamed. "How?" she screamed. "He was at the hospital when he was snatched. I hacked his phone and turned on the camera and saw the entire thing." Adrian explained. He takes out his phone and shows the video he recorded. "I recorded everything the kidnapper said as leverage for blackmail." he said with a creepy smile.

Slowly taking the phone from his hand, Michaela views the video. She watched as the woman talked to someone in the background. Michaela heard faint dragging and thought that it might be Cody. It was gut-wrenching to watch.

Suddenly, Michaela does a double-take when she recognizes the woman. "I've seen her," she whispered. "She was that reporter lady . . . when Takanawa . . ." Michaela wasn't able to finish because Adrian snatched the phone from her grasp. He stares at the woman's face before looking back at Michaela. "Are you sure?" he asked. "Positive." Michaela answered shakily.

A low growl rumbled in Adrian's chest. "Then she obviously isn't a real reporter. But maybe harder to kill if she knew how to take down Cody." he said. "Though she doesn't seem smart with technology. You should've seen her face when I texted her saying I saw her." he laughed.

'This guy is mental,' Michaela thought. "I'm not gonna ask how you hacked Cody's phone. But I will ask how the hell we are suppose to get Cody back from his crazy uncle!?" she yelled exasperatedly. "Simple, we go to his business building, sneak in, find Cody, and kill Michael." Adrian said as if it was some walk in the park. "Uh, I don't know where you are from. But this isn't some damn movie! This is real life!" Michaela yelled. "Quit your yelling! I know how to sneak into places undetected. We'll find Cody before anything happens to him." Adrian said surely.

"Then we better hurry. Who knows what's happening to Cody right now."

Chapter 22

C ody

It felt like his neck was being squished till it hurt to breathe or move. He kept his head down to keep himself from feeling pain. Also so that he did not have to look at his captors.Those bastards kept staring at him like he was a piece of meat. They looked crazier than Adrian or Michaela when she's craving a bloody movie.

He recognized the woman that kidnapped him. That damn so called reporter. No wonder he's never seen her before on television. And the man beside her was the camera man. They both were armed with guns hanging at their waist. Ready to attack if necessary.

When Cody came too, he found himself in a room full of nice furniture with white tile floors. Only downside, he was chained to the wall. And Michael was staring at him with a dark gleeful look on his face. His face had changed drastically since the last time Cody has seen him. Scars covered his face that must've taken many amounts of makeup to cover.

"Evening, boy. Glad to see you're awake." Michael said with fake happiness.

"I knew it! You were there!" Cody immediately said with triumph, but not forgetting the fact that he was in chains. Michael glared at Cody but doesn't do anything. "I had a feeling you'd recognize me. Sorry for the childhood trauma." he said with no sign of remorse. A growl was Cody's response toward Michael. "You killed my parents! Now I'll fucking kill you!" Cody hissed.

First, there was surprise in Michael's eyes. Then it became humorous as he started to laugh. "Kill me? You can't even reach me!" Michael laughed.

With a sudden surge of adrenaline, Cody pushes himself off the ground and lunges at Michael. The chains were long enough for him to be a foot away. When he reached the end of the chain, Cody swung his leg up and struck Michael in the knee. There was a loud crack as Michael's leg bent the wrong way. Cody watched as his uncle fell to his one good knee with a scream.

The pain in Michael's eyes made Cody smile. He laughed at him. But it was cut off when two hands clench down on his throat. Cody grabbed his attacker's hands and tried to pry him off. Through fuzzing eyes, he could see it was Michael strangling him.

Cody clawed at Michael's face and his nails scraped down his cheeks. "Ahh!" Michael screamed. He lets go of Cody and limps away. There was blood running down his cheeks. "Bastard!" Michael yelled angrily. "Keep him here! I'll be right back!" he growled before limping out of the room.

Small droplets of blood dripped to the floor. It gave Cody a sense of pride.

And Cody is where he is now. Chained up, throat swollen, and stuck in a room with armed people. 'How am I going to get out of this mess?' Cody thought. He thought of Michaela, Sarah, and even Adrian. None of them knew where he was. Well—maybe Michaela and Adrian know. The two know of Michael's plan. But they didn't know when Michael would strike.

His ears catch the sound of the door opening. He doesn't look up to see who entered. Best guess was the bastard. The hairs on the back of neck stood on end as he felt eyes on him.

"Is the kid awake?" asked Michael. He sounded very agitated as he walked into the room. "Been awake the entire time." answered the woman.

Cody picks up his head with a hiss as he looked directly at Michael. His face was red from the scrapes and dried blood was stuck to his skin. (Not an attractive look.) Michael's leg was wrapped up but it wasn't enough from the sound of the crack Cody heard. He would need a cast, not a simple wrap-up.

"You're looking better," Cody sneered with a hoarse voice.

Those eyes that were the same as his father's glared darkly at Cody. "If these scar over, I'm gonna kill you harder than I planned." Michael growled. "You already have ugly scars. Did my mom give you those or my dad?" Cody asked.

"Elisa has always been a tough woman." Michael said with an adoring smile. "I wish she married me and not that bastard." he said.

God, I think I'm going to vomit, Cody thought. "My mom loved my father! No way in hell she would fall for a man like you!" he shouted. Then, he finds his head snapping to the side. His cheek burned heavily and stung around the edges. "Fuck you." Michael growled.

"Sir, if I may remind you, we need him undamaged for him to sign the papers." spoke up the woman. She looked slightly worried but didn't seem to show it to Michael or Cody.

Suddenly, there were screams and gunshots coming from below them. The floor vibrated from the gunfire. "What the hell?" Michael hissed. He turns toward the woman and male and says,"Go and see what it is."

"Yes sir," the two said in unison before leaving the room.

Cody felt his hope lift. It has to be Adrian, he thought. It has to be.

Chapter 23

A drian

AN HOUR BEFORE

The wig was itchy as hell and the suit he wore was ridiculously tight. It felt like he was in some torture device. He shifted uncomfortably in the chair as he waited for Michaela.

Tapping his foot against the floor, he absentmindedly pets Marcella. He hated waiting. The more time he waited, the less time he risks losing Cody. How long do girls fucking get ready? Adrian thought annoyed. He rubs his jacket, feeling for his knife and gun for some assurance.

"How do I look?" Michaela asked as she enters the room.

Turning around from where he sat on the couch, he sees a different woman. Her hair was disguised with a blond wig. She dressed herself up in brown trousers and a white blouse with a light green cardigan. "Do I look like a boring business lady?" Michaela asked as she spun on her two-inch, green heels. "Wouldn't give you a second glance," Adrian commented.

Despite it barely being a compliment, Michaela laughed. "Gotta fit the profile to be able to sneak in, don't I?" she asked before collecting her purse. "Don't forget to keep this with you," Adrian said as he hands her a switchblade. "Incase you're found out."

The light mood she had disappeared. She takes the knife reluctantly and stuffs it in her bra. "If this wasn't a life or death situation, I'd find this kinda fun." she said to try and lighten the mood. "I'll be laughing when I kill the bastards who took Cody." Adrian said darkly.

Fear flashes in her eyes at his reply. "I-I'll go get the car ready. We can go over the plan on the way." Michaela said shakily as she takes her car-keys out of her purse. Then she scurries out of the house.

Adrian sighed as he slowly got off the couch. He rubs Marcella's head before he heads to the front door. There were so many disadvantages to this, he knew that. Allowing a girl who knows nothing of spying to help him. But he knows that she can help him as reinforcements. Extra muscle.

He passes a mirror that stood a few feet from the door. The sight of the black haired wig sent a chill down his spine. The color was the same as it was before. Adrian inherited his father's hair, the reason he permanently dyed his hair red. He wanted to forget his father for all he has done.

Now he's back to the same color, even if it was a wig. It sent a boiling rage up his stomach as he stared at his reflection. Letting out a growl, Adrian finally leaves the house.

Snow was actually falling. It was only flurrying and wasn't covering the ground just yet. Adrian stared up at the sky, allowing the small specks to fall on his face. 'Wonder how much blood will fall after tonight.' he thinks as he walks over to the car.

Adrian slips into the passenger seat and shuts the door. "Drive." he ordered. Michaela nods and backs out of the driveway. She turns left and drives down the street. "So how are we supposed to get Cody? He may not be at Michael's building." Michaela said. "He will." Adrian stated. He knows what people like Michael think. They would keep their captives in plain sight.

Michaela decided not to say anything as she got on to a busy street.

The silence between the two was becoming uncomfortable. Adrian was playing with his knife, staring at the clean blade. "When we get there. Be prepared for anything. There's a possibility that they know who you are so you can't let them realize it's you.

"Don't make direct contact if you encounter Michael or that woman. Keep a low profile, stay calm. When the time is right, I need you to make a distraction so I can scope out the place to find Cody. I'll have to remind you that this may get very bloody." Adrian explained.

They reached a red light when Michaela replied,"I know the risks. Just promise me that you will get Cody back."

"I will." Adrian replied, and that ended the conversation.

The drive was painstakingly long with traffic when it should've taken about twenty minutes. Almost an hour at most. They reached Michael's building, which they realized was corporate building Lawyer and Finance. One of the most expensive corporations in New York City.

"Michael works here?! If we kill him this will become more serious than what he did to Cody!" Michaela said as she started to panic. Adrian could tell she was having second thoughts. He grabs her arms and makes her look at him. "Michaela," he said as he looked at her dead in the eyes. "Cody needs our help. I already have enough evidence on him if this goes south."

There was still some hesitance on Michaela's face, but she still nodded. "Okay," she said. "Lets do this."

NOW

Adrian walked in a minute before Michaela does. He viewed the lobby and spots the reception desk that is a few paces from the elevators. There were a few security guards walking around. He spots a few security cameras and could tell he can't just sneak in.

He heads toward the reception desk as Michaela entered the building. The glasses he wore let him see her reflection. She walked toward a bunch of chairs in the waiting area. Adrian could see her twitching from twenty feet away.

When she sits down, Michaela takes out Adrian's computer and began to type. Beginning stage one . . .

"Excuse me?" Adrian said to the receptionist.

The receptionist was a young male, probably close to Adrian's age. Short blond hair, shaven face, and had a good build with big shoulders. He picked up his head to look at Adrian with a questioning look. "Hello. I am here to talk to Mr. Winters." Adrian said calmly and professionally. "Do you have an appointment?" the receptionist asked. "I'm pretty sure I do. The company I work at said they set an appointment." Adrian said.

"Let me check," the receptionist as he began to type on his computer. Just then, Adrian's phone rang in his jacket pocket.

Quickly checking his phone, he reads what the text said.

Ten seconds. Get ready.

Adrian doesn't turn to look at Michaela but fixes his glasses as a signal. He looks back at the receptionist and waits for his cue.

"THAT ASSHOLE!" suddenly shrieks out Michaela. Beginning stage two . . .

All heads turned around to face Michaela, who abruptly stands up and sends the chair she sat on fall backwards. Fury could be seen in her eyes as she stared at 'her' computer. "After all I've done for him and he fucking cheats on me!" Michaela roared. 'Not bad acting,' Adrian thought impressed.

Picking up 'her' computer, she smashes it to the ground. "I will kill him!" Michaela screamed. 'Good thing I have two computers,' Adrian thought with a cringe. He notices the security guards were beginning to advance toward her. Quickly, Adrian got into action.

He excuses himself from the reception desk and walks toward Michaela. "Ma'am, please calm down," he said. "You're causing a scene." Adrian sets his hand on Michaela's shoulder and was then punched in the face.

'Shit! The bitch can pack a punch!'

Stumbling backwards, Adrian held his nose at he felt blood drip out of his nostrils. He watches as the security guards grabs Michaela and drag her out of the building. 'Hope you remember the rest,' Adrian thought as he wipes his nose with his sleeve. "Are you alright, sir?" asked a female security guard. She examines his bleeding nose with a cringing face.

"I'm alright. Is it okay if I may go to the bathroom?" Adrian asked as he held his nose up. "Of course." she said as she guides him to the bathroom.

They passed the reception desk and elevators. Luckily, the boy's bathroom was the closest to the elevators. "Thank you," Adrian said with a smile toward the security guard before he entered the bathroom. He grabs paper towels from the dispenser and cleans his nose. "Michaela has a good punch." he said aloud.

After wiping his face clean of blood, Adrian checks the bathroom for any people inside. 'All clear. Beginning stage three.' He takes off his jacket and stuffs it in his suitcase. 'If I read the blueprints correctly, Michael's office should be on the 25th floor.' he thought as he checks his weapons. 'Two knives strapped to my ankles, a gun tucked into my waist, and a blade hidden in my jeans.' Adrian listed.

Taking off his glasses, Adrian reaches to grab his wig but stops. 'Best to stay hidden for now,' he thinks as he leaves the bathroom.

He quickly pushes the elevator button, and luckily it opens immediately. There was no one inside. Adrian began to tap the twenty-fifth floor button. Just as the doors shut, his phone rang. He takes out his phone and sees it was a text message from Michaela.

I'll be coming in soon. Hope you'll get rid of any goons before I get there.

I always get them done.

Taking in a deep breath, Adrian pockets his phone and prepares for what may be beyond the door. He takes out a small device he stuck to the bottom of his watch. With one small push, the device began to beep.

Once it began to beep, he takes off the wig. "Lets get this started." Adrian said in a dark tone as the doors opened to the twenty-fifth floor.

The elevator opened to a long hallway. Adrian's senses rose high when he didn't see anyone. He carefully steps out of the elevator and began to walk down the hallway. His hands were stuffed in his pockets but his thumbs brush against his gun.

The sound of his footsteps were light but echoing. Any chance of hiding was out the door. Anyone could hear him come in.

A person suddenly steps out of one of the rooms that stood on the right of the hallway. It was a very buff man, taller than Adrian, and threatening looking. But Adrian has taken down scarier. He turned his head and spotted Adrian. "Who are you?" he demanded.

"Just here for Michael. But mainly Cody." Adrian responded calmly as he takes out his gun and fires. The bullet hit the man in the neck and exited through the other side. Blood sprayed all over the floor as he fell to the ground dead. Dark glee gleamed in Adrian's eyes as he walked up to the dead body. He has never rescued anyone but if it means killing people, he's just fine doing it.

Snatching a keycard from the dead man's hand, Adrian pockets it in his jeans. 'Hopefully, this will open to whatever room Cody is in,' he thought as he stepped over the body and continued on his way. He begins to whistle a tune out of boredom.

There were footsteps storming down one of the hallways that connects to the hallway Adrian was in. He cocks his gun in front of him in preparation.

Three different individuals ran around the corner. All were armed with guns. But they weren't ready for Adrian. He fires three rounds that hit their marks. The two to the sides fell with bullet holes in their head while the middle one fell with only a chest wound. Still alive.

A sneer grew on Adrian's face as he walked up to the wounded guard. It was an older African American male. His head was shaven to a buzz and his skin was riddled with scars. Probably from a war because he would be described as a soldier. Grabbing the man by his shirt, Adrian pulls him up into a sitting position. Blood pumped out of the wound faster as the man moved.

"Listen to me, and listen closely," Adrian says as he pressed the hot barrel of his gun against the man's throat. "Tell me where you are holding Cody." he finished darkly. He bared his teeth at the man like a predator ready to attack. "D-Down the . . . the hall. Office has . . . secret room behind . . . bookshelf." The man barely managed to finish his sentences. Blood slipped through his lips, and he couldn't stop coughing, causing blood to splatter on Adrian's face.

"At least your death won't be in vain." Adrian said as he takes out a knife. "Close your eyes. That's all I'll say." he whispered as he sets the tip of the blade on the man's throat.

With a single nod, the man closes his eyes and waits. 'Night night,' Adrian thought as he slipped the knife through the man's throat. The tension in the man's body disappeared and he dies instantly.

Adrian's phone vibrated again as he stood up. He checked the message as he walked down the hallway.

On my way up. Get rid of the guards yet?

Four. Better mind the blood.

He stuffs his phone into his back pocket as reaches the office. The door was closed, and for all he knew, someone could be inside. Adrian checks the magazine case to make sure he had enough bullets left. Only one round left, better make it count, Adrian thought as he checked the case before resetting it back in the gun.

As quietly as he could, Adrian opens the door with one hand and a gun raised in the other. He peeks in and saw no one inside. Taking in a deep breath, Adrian enters the room and began to search.

A big desk stood in the center of the room with a flat screen tv hung up on the wall behind it. Two chairs stood in front of the desk, a table was standing at the left side of the room and had bottles of alcohol on top. Adrian spots a big bookcase standing on the right side of the table. It was filled with books but the edges of the case, he could see the blackness of a corridor.

He stealthy walks across the room and reaches the book-case. But before he could move it, it moves on its own. Adrian jumps three feet back as the bookcase is pushed back. A man and a woman stepped through the doorway.

Adrian froze when he recognizes the woman as the one who took Cody. The same woman he saw on the phone. The bitch that pretended to be that reporter.

A feral growl rumbled through Adrian's chest as he stuffs his gun into the back of his jeans and throws one of his knives. Sadly, the woman caught sight of the knife and ducks before it could hit her. Instead, the man is stabbed in the throat. He slumps to the ground, letting out bloody gurgles as his life left his body.

Dumbstruck, the woman looks down at her partner then at Adrian. "Who are you?" she demanded as she aims her gun at him. "I told you I could see you." Adrian said amusingly. Realization flashes across the woman's face. "You were the one who sent that text message?" It was more of an accusation than a question.

"Guilty as charged." Adrian said with a fake bow. As he bowed, he attacks.

The woman tried to fire but fumbles with the trigger. She got stabbed in the chest. Adrian covered her mouth to keep her from screaming. His lips brush her ear as he says,"Next time, don't take what's mine." Then he lets her fall.

She fell down beside her cohort with the knife still stuck in her chest. The lifelessness in her eyes gave Adrian pride. He grabs the two knives and pulls them out of the bodies. "I'll be taking these back," he said as he wipes the blood off with his jeans.

'Michael, you're next,' Adrian thought as he stared at the dark staircase where the woman had come from.

Chapter 24

Cody

The gunshots stopped and everything went still. There were no screams, no voices to hear.

He couldn't scream because his mouth was taped shut. But he made sure to make noise by banging his chains against the ground. Both fear and relief was running through Cody. For all he knew, it could be Adrian or someone else that is out for Michael's head.

He rubs the chains against the floor to make a grinding noise. The chains cut into his wrists to the point of bleeding. It hurt like hell but he refused to stop. He had to find a way to get free because he knew that Michael was hiding in waiting.

Through the grinding noises Cody was making, he heard footsteps. He stopped in mid-rub and listened closely. His ears straining to hear anything.

The door to the room creaked open very slowly. Cody's stopped breathing as he waited for whoever or whatever to enter.

A familiar redhead peers through the opening. He crept into the room with barely a sound. Cody noticed the amount of blood on Adrian's person and was afraid to know how many people had died. But his fear changed to panic when he remembers Adrian was walking into a trap.

"Mmmm! Mmhhnmmm!" Cody tried to scream through the tape but could only hum.

The murderer looked up when he heard Cody. A relieved smile grew on his face as he quickly crossed the room to get to Cody. 'No! It's a trap!' Cody thought as he pulled against his chains. Adrian didn't notice Cody's weak warnings as he got down on his knees and pulled the tape off Cody's mouth.

"Are you alright, love?" Adrian asked as he held Cody's face in his hands. "It's a trap!" Cody screamed in Adrian's face.

Realization crossed Adrian's face, but it was too late. He was hit on the side of the head with Michael's gun.

"ADRIAN!" Cody screamed in horror.

Adrian's face was already swelling from the hit as he laid on the ground groaning. Blood dripped down his nose and some even came out of his eye.

"I don't know who you are but you made a big mistake coming here." Michael sneered. He was about to shoot Adrian, but he was kicked very hard in the bad knee. He fell to the ground with a painful crunch coming from his leg.

A growl ripped through Adrian's throat as he lunges at Michael. He takes out one of his knives and slashes it at Michael's face. Quickly, Michael raised his arms to block the attack. His clothes tore as the knife slipped through the clothes and cut into his skin. Blood squirted out of the cuts and sprayed all over Adrian's face.

Insane laughter escaped Adrian as he pushed Michael to the ground. "Never take my Cody from me!" he yelled in

Michael's face. He held Michael down and raises the knife above his head.

Cody watched in horror as he prepares to see a murder appear in front of him. He didn't care for Michael but he didn't want to have another childhood trauma. His throat was clamped shut, he couldn't say anything. He couldn't look away.

Before Adrian could finish Michael, a gun suddenly fired . . .

The knife falls from Adrian's grasp as he fell off of Michael. Blood was pooling out of his stomach as he laid there. "NO!" Cody screamed hoarsely.

Soon, crazed laughter escaped Michael as he stood up with his leg in an even worse position than before. "This piece of shit thought he could kill me? Ha!" he laughed. He kicked Adrian but winces from the pain in his leg. "You bastard! I will kill you!" Cody screamed angrily. He pulls against his chains, snarling like an animal. "I won't allow you to get away with this!" Cody shouted.

He tries to reach for Adrian but the chains were too short. His fingers barely grazed Adrian's body.

Suddenly, his eyes catch sight of a key that was in Adrian's hand. He held it tightly in his fist to keep Michael from seeing it. Cody looks between Michael and the key. 'It has to be the key to the chains. Smart boy,' Cody thought as he inches forward.

"You know what, Cody? You remind me more and more of your father. Same determination, looks, and smarts. It's just sickening." Michael said grossly. He shifts his gun in between his hands. "Only thing that is different is your thirst for blood." he said with a laugh. "If you really wish to kill me, how are you going to do that? Your only chance of escape is dead and you're practically immobilized." he stated.

Cody kept his eyes on Michael as he slowly reaches for the key. He waited for the right moment to snatch it without Michael seeing. His fingers touch Adrian's skin and his heart leaped when he felt warmth.

"You know I was going to kill you that night as well? But I changed my mind at the last second because I needed to have the money transferred to me properly. The money would've just gone back to my father, and I would never have it. I couldn't lose it all so easily."

'Someone shut him up,' Cody thought before snatching the key when Michael looked away. Happily cheering in his mind that he can escape.

Suddenly, Adrian began to move. He slowly began to move his arms and legs. His chest moved quick with short breaths. 'Thank goodness,' Cody thought relieved. Quickly, he begins to unlock the chains, trying to be as quiet as possible. 'Keep fighting, Adrian. I'll get us out of here.' Cody thought.

"You won't get away with this, Michael. Sarah will notice I'm missing, and she'll put two and two together!" Cody said intently. He hears a faint click as the cuff on his left wrist came off. He grabs the chains before it fell and could cause any noise. Holding his breath as he waited for Michael to respond if he did hear him.

"Your foster mother won't notice anything. I'll tell her that you decided to move in with me. And if that doesn't work, I'll kill her as well." Michael said with a shrug.

It felt like he was shot straight in the heart. White hot fury built up inside of Cody as he unlocks the last of his restraints. He didn't bother to stop the chains from making noise. The second he stood, Michael turned around. "I will not let you kill Sarah!" Cody roared before he runs full speed at Michael. Michael's eyes grew wide as he raises his gun to fire.

Cody's instincts kicked in and he dives down and rolls. Gunshots fired, and he felt the bullets whiz by his head. When he lands back on his feet, Cody throws himself at Michael and tackles him off his feet. His head hits the wall behind them and causes cracks to spread up the wall like spiderwebs. As Michael was in disorientation, Cody grabs the gun from his uncle's hand and stuffs it in Michael's mouth.

"Must hurt doesn't it? I may have been strangled but being bashed against the your—what is that? Sheetrock? Marble? Whatever—it must've hurt like hell." Cody said with dark amusement. "I dunno what my parents did to you, but I hope this hurts you more than what you did to them." he said as he pulls the trigger.

Only, no bullets flew. There were only clicking noises coming from the gun. "What the hell?" Cody thought aloud. "Ran out of bullets, what luck." Michael sneered as he punches Cody in the cheek.

Stumbling back a few steps, Cody was proceeded with punches to the chest and face. He braced himself for every hit, being used to being beaten by bullies all his life. Compared to the bullies, Michael was actually trying to kill him unlike the rest.

Cody trips on Adrian's discarded knife and fell flat on his back. Pain shot up his spine and made his head ring. His eyes become hazy and he saw twos. 'Can't die now. Not now,' Cody thought as he tried to stand up. He felt a foot push against his chest and pushed Cody back down to the floor.

"I have a good forger on call so I won't be needing your signature. With all this damn problems you're giving me, I'll just do that. I won't be needing your damn signature." Michael said darkly. Cody's vision cleared and he looks up at his uncle. He laughed with blood slipping through his lips at how busted up Michael's face looked. "Whether I die or not. You'll be in hell. I'll haunt your damn ass till you die." Cody sneered.

"I don't believe in ghosts." Michael said.

"You should believe in guardian angels," Cody began with a smirk. "Because I have one." he finished.

Just as Cody said it, Michael suddenly gasps. His eyes grew as wide as saucers, pain clearly seen in them. He drops his gun and slowly sank down to the floor. "Take that, bastard." spoke Michaela from behind. She backs away from Michael with a bloody knife in her hands. Cody could see that she was shaken, but there was still determination in her eyes.

Gurgles escaped Michael as blood began to spill out of his mouth. Then he collapses on the ground with a thump. No signs of life.

With a groan, Cody stood back up. He didn't spare Michael's body a glance as he walked over to Michaela. When he reached her, he pulls Michaela into a tight hug. "I'm so glad you're alright." Cody whispered in her ear. Soon, Michaela returned the hug with a stronger amount of force. "I'm glad you're alive," she said shakily. "But I can't believe I just killed a man," she added with a hiccup.

"If you two are gonna be yapping all day, I'm gonna bleed out over here!" spoke up Adrian with an irritated yet tired tone.

Realization hit Cody like a ton of bricks. Quickly, he lets go of Michaela and hurries over to Adrian. "Shit! Sorry!" Cody hissed. "Oh no problem. I'm just dying here." Adrian said as he slowly sat up. His entire shirt was covered in blood, yet Cody couldn't tell who's blood it is. His usual pale complexion became a deathly color, and his eyes somehow grew brighter than duller.

"How are you still alive?" Michaela asked exasperatedly. She took off her blazer and handed it to Cody for him to use it to cover Adrian's wound. "Gee, thanks," Adrian said sarcastically but weakly. "Enough talking! We need to get you to a hospital!" Cody said.

With all his strength, Cody dragged Adrian back to his feet. "Michaela, call an ambulance." Cody ordered. He throws Adrian's arm over his shoulder and began to walk them both to the door. His own legs were weak from the abuse but he refused to show discomfort.

"I can't go to a hospital, Cody. They'll arrest me." Adrian said for once in desperation. "Not if they don't know it's you. We'll find a way to get you help." Cody assured him, giving Adrian a soft smile. The two boys' eyes met and both of their pain seemed to disappear.

Suddenly, Michaela screams.

Cody and Adrian turn around in surprise and saw a still alive Michael holding Michaela captive. He had one of his arms wrapped around her neck while the other held a knife that was pressed against her chest. "No one is going any-where!" he said insanely. The most wildest look was on his face that could rival Adrian.

"You," Michael said as he pointed at Cody,"are going to fucking sign those papers and I'm gonna get the money! Or this girl," he gestured at Michaela with a squeeze,"will die." Tears were spilling down Michaela's face as she tried to fight Michaela, but it was no use because he was stronger. She tried biting his arm but he responded with a squeeze to her neck.

Slowly, Cody backs away from Adrian but kept a firm hand on Adrian's back to keep him standing. "Michael, don't do this. There is no need to hurt Michaela." Cody said carefully. He could see that Michael was a ticking time bomb. At any moment he could explode.

"Sign the papers and I'll let her go." Michael said. "Don't do it, Cody! I'll happily die if it means you get your birthright!" Michaela said with a shaky smile.

"You won't be the one to die, Michaela." Cody assured her. He reaches into the back of Adrian's pants and grabs the gun. "He is." he said before whipping the gun out and fires.

Silence overcame them as Cody watches Michael let go of Michaela and fall with blood coming out of the bullet hole in his eye. Cody stared at his uncle's body, the dread he had felt for years finally lifted off his shoulders. Finally, his parents' deaths have been avenged.

His arm that held the gun was shaking tremendously. He just killed a man. And despite the shaking, he loved it. Cody loved the way it felt taking Michael's life away.

"Nice shot." Adrian said, breaking the silence. He then grabs Cody's face and kissed him. Blood was mixed between the saliva but Cody could care less. Right now, he needed something to take his mind off this damn nightmare. "Make-out when you're both healed up and alone. Also, we need to get the hell out of here." Michaela said. She looks through the window that Cody has never noticed. A very worried look was on her face as she looked down. "The cops are here." she stated.

Chapter 25

Cody

The flashes of cameras and loud voices were giving him a headache. Every flash felt like a mini explosion. Every word made the headache grow even worse. The reporters kept demanding for him to answer their questions. It was Minnesota all over again. (Except these reporters were way worse than the ones back then. The reporters in Minnesota weren't as crazy.)

Michaela, Adrian, and Cody weren't able to evade the police even if they tried. With both Adrian and Cody's injuries, they couldn't move. Also that Adrian fell unconscious from blood loss just moments before the police bursted into the room.

The rest went by as a dull blur in Cody's case. They were all grabbed and taken out of the building to be examined. Michaela and Cody were handcuffed while officers stayed with Adrian to wait for the EMTs. The sight of Adrian's lifeless-looking body sent dread through Cody. He never thought he'd hold feelings for the crazy murderer in such a short time. But he did.

Cody had to step over the bodies of the ones who kidnapped him. No signs of remorse on his face when he accidentally trips over the woman's head. I hope it was painful, bitch, Cody thought.

The stares he got from policemen and policewomen weren't like the ones back in Minnesota. Those ones held remorse and pity. These showed suspicion and question. Just what happened to him? What did he do?

The hallway was covered in blood and dead bodies. A total of four people, not counting Michael or the other two. All were heavily armed to the teeth. How exactly did Adrian get them all without getting a scratch on him? Cody thought.

Voices echoed all around Cody as he was dragged out of the elevator and into the lobby. There were reporters all over to place trying to get answers. When they caught sight of Cody and Michaela, it was like a wave crashing on them. The policemen that were escorting them had to push the reporters back with their batons.

He and Michaela were directed to two different ambulances to be examined. A female EMT checks on Cody's vitals before looking at his bruises. Sadly, he knew the procedure. He was irritated but kept calm and follows every direction he was given. The EMT gently touches the bruises on Cody's neck and it made him since in pain. Everything was still very raw to the point that Cody thinks his skin might split.

It felt like hours till Adrian was wheeled outside via stretcher. He was still knocked out cold. From where Cody stood, he could see how pale Adrian has become. 'You shouldn't have gotten involved with a guy like me, Adrian.'

"CODY! WHERE ARE YOU? WHERE IS MY SON?"

If Cody was in an anime, he would be sweat-dropping or close to face-planting on the ground. He has never seen an angry Sarah before, and it looks like a lightning storm is heading his way. And whoever is in front of her is gonna get hit. Hard.

He looks toward the large crowd and saw Sarah pushing her way through. She was in her black chef uniform and looked completely disheveled. Cody could see her mascara was running down her cheeks from where he stood. 'Hell is about to break loose in, three, two, one.' Cody counted down.

Sarah breaks free from the crowd-control officers and ran toward Cody. She had that look that meant someone is going to die. Usually, Cody would be hiding upstairs with Izzy while Sarah was exploding. But now, there was no way he can hide.

"Restrain her!" suddenly ordered a familiar voice.

'Son of a bitch,' Cody thought as he looked toward Detective Jackson. Unlike the day Cody first met him, Jackson looked like he hasn't slept in days. Dark circles hung under his eyes and his clothes looked like they haven't been washed in awhile. All in all, he hasn't been taking care of himself.

"I want to know why my son is handcuffed! Why was I called to be informed that he is involved in a fucking murder?!" Sarah yelled as she elbowed her way out of the grasp of a male officer's arms. She stomped her way toward Detective Jackson with a fire in her eyes. "Give me answers now or I'll sue your asses for this!" Sarah threatened.

Detective Jackson gave Sarah a hard look as he says,"He was found in a room with a dead man and had blood all over him!"

"I was kidnapped by my own uncle! He fucking tried to kill me!" Cody snapped. He lightly shoves the EMT away and gets in Jackson's face. "I'm the damn victim! I was just defending myself! But I doubt you'd believe me because Michael is a damn CEO of some big business!" he screamed in Jackson's face. Anger he never knew he had just exploded that moment. "He killed my parents. I don't care if you believe me but it's the truth." Cody growled.

The hardness on Jackson's face changed to a look on pity. His eyes shifted to his feet for a moment before looking back up at Cody. But before he could say anything, there was a loud screech of tires.

An ambulance truck went speeding passed them and toward the crowd. It's lights were flashing and sirens blaring. People screamed in horror before jumping out of the way.

The ambulance truck ran over the barriers and through the separated crowd. No one was hit, and police were shooting at the vehicle's tires. Whoever drove the truck was smart and swerved side go side to avoid the bullets. They hit a few police cruisers to get through the parking lot. Then they reached the street and drove away.

Cody had a feeling that he knew who was behind the wheel. 'Crazy bastard,' he thought. 'God, I love him,' he thought amusingly. He looks at Jackson and saw the most horrific look on his face. "Chase down that fucking ambulance! Don't kill the driver but subdue them!" Jackson barked out orders.

"Can we go home, officer? Cody has been through a rough day and I want him to forget all of this." Sarah said. Her eyes drift over to Michaela, and Cody could see surprise appear in her eyes. 'Guess they didn't tell her about Michaela', he thought. The look on Sarah's face switches to authority as she says," And Id like to have her come with us!"

Jackson turns his attention back to Sarah, and he looked more annoyed than he was before. "I can't release suspects! They need to be questioned." he said. "You can ask them tomorrow. Right now, they need rest." Sarah snapped. "Michaela, come here, please." she called out with less hostility to Michaela. "Listen, you can't just take away these two!" Jackson yelled. "I'm not taking them away. You can come get them in the morning." Sarah said calmly.

'Way to go, Sarah,' Cody said with a big smile. He sees Michaela walk up to them with an officer at her side. She no longer looked afraid, instead she was happy. Cody understood why, she doesn't have to be scared. The worse was behind them.

"Lets go, kids," Sarah said as she grabs Cody and Sarah's wrists and drags them away from Detective Jackson. As they walked away, Cody could feel Jackson's gaze. He turns his head to look back at Jackson with a smirk. "See you tomorrow, Detective Jackson! Can't wait to meet Detective Johns again!" Cody said as he waves tauntingly at Jackson.

Chapter 26

Adrian

It took about thirty minutes to escape the police. He veered through lanes with his foot pressed fully on the gas pedal. The screams of frightened citizens barely affected him. Of course, he tried not to hit any one because he wasn't that heartless.

When he makes a turn a block away from the police, he quickly ditched the ambulance truck. Luckily, there wasn't anyone on the street or sidewalks. He jumped out of the truck and took off running after he rolled. As he ran through an alley, he heard the ambulance truck crash. Then there was the rushing sound of a fire hydrant exploding. Luckily, he grabbed a bag full of narcotics and other medicines to treat himself before jumping.

His wounds began to throb tremendously as he walks. He was lucky that Michael didn't shoot him in the chest. The bullet passed through his stomach and exited through his back. It didn't puncture any organs so it was the lack of blood that was life threatening. Adrian recalled falling unconscious just as he saw the police bursting into the room, and he woke up inside an ambulance truck with EMTs staring down at him.

The distance wails of sirens made him quicken his step. He was five blocks away from his apartment and thirty miles from Cody's house. Through his haze, he saw Cody being handcuffed and questioned. If Adrian fled and returned to Cody's house, there would obviously be officers there. Cody had enough in his hands, and no one needs to know one of his friends is a murderer.

'Hope Cody and Michaela can handle interrogation. Wait, no, the other way around.' Adrian thought amusingly.

He felt his stitches begin to throb, and Adrian knew they were becoming undone. Breathing was starting to become a pain even when he stopped running. Adrian rests his back against the brick wall and coughed up blood-filled saliva. "Should lay off . . . the running." he said to himself.

Slowly, he unzips the bag with a shaky hand. It was filled with medicine and gauze. Taking in a deep breath, Adrian rolls up the jacket he stole to look at his stitches. His wound had swelled up in size with the stitches barely holding together. The pain in the wound was becoming unbearable. Adrian searches through the bag for any narcotics that would ease the pain.

He finds a syringe and a small vile full of morphine. With shaky hands, he fills the syringe full of morphine. Then he sinks the needle into the bullet wound and injects the morphine into his body. It felt like a flower was blooming in his stomach. The pain eased from the wound, and Adrian could see his skin slowly settle from the swelling.

'Just five blocks to go. Five blocks,' Adrian tried to think encouragingly. He pushes himself back onto his feet with a groan. There was still pain sizzling in his bones but it didn't bother him as much. Taking in a deep breath, Adrian holds the bag close to his back and walks away.

Never has Adrian felt so drowsy in his life. It took less than ten minutes for the morphine to spread through his entire body. Luckily, there was no longer any pain in his stitches or bruises. But it was now difficult to walk straight without something to press against.

His head pounded with drowsiness as he walked down the empty sidewalk. It was almost two in the morning. Not even drunk men or women were outside.

Through drowsy eyes, he read the street sign when he reaches an intersection. 'Baker Street. Great. Two more blocks to go,' Adrian thought with a groan. In all his years of being on the run, never has he felt such hatred for his mother to making him this way.

Faintly, Adrian hears the echoing sound of police sirens. The large empty street seemed to grow smaller as the police car starts to drive down the block. Adrian cursed as he slips behind a dumpster. He squatted down to shrink into the darkness. Small shocks of pain shot through his stomach as he curls himself up.

After what felt like forever, a squad car drove by. It's lights were flashing bright enough to cause a seizure. Adrian kept his head down and waited quietly. Despite barely feeling anything, he could feel the tension in his bones as he was prepared for anything.

Once he could no longer hear the sirens, Adrian gets back on his feet, but suddenly, he feels sickness rush through him. He felt the last bit of food flow back up his throat and he couldn't hold it in. Collapsing back on to his knees, Adrian threw up everything he had. 'If I could, I would've brought Michael back from the dead just to kill him myself!'

Five minutes of constant retching, he could feel his head getting ready to explode. "Fuck my life." Adrian said in between hacks.

"Your life must've sucked if you say that." suddenly spoke a woman from behind. It was surprisingly familiar but Adrian couldn't put his finger on it. He coughed a few times before looking up.

There was an older woman standing a few feet away. She was dressed in an evening gown that said she came back from a fancy dinner or ball or something. The shadows hid her face yet Adrian felt like he knew her. "You don't know the half of it." he said with a wipe at his chin. His words received a laugh from the woman, and then it became clear.

Her laugh was the same. Her form was the same. Even her hair was the same. Adrian went rigid when he recognized who she was. The very woman that left him so long ago . . .

"Mother." he hissed.

Almost immediately, his mother stopped laughing. Even though her face was hid by the darkness, Adrian knew there was horror in her eyes. "I don't have a son." she lied. It made Adrian laugh cruelly and insanely. He slowly got back to his feet despite the nausea. Through his bangs, he looked directly at his mother.

"Maria Blue. Cheated on loving husband, and then left his ass with an eight-year old son." Adrian said darkly. He pulls back his hoodie to reveal his face to his mother. "I wonder if you know that Frank is dead, Mother? Did you bother to go to his funeral?" he asked curiously.

Maria began to shake in what could be either fear or anger. "I don't have a son." she repeated. "Bullshit!" Adrian shouted.

In a blink of an eye, he grabs his mother and slams her into the brick wall. His hands dug into her shoulders till they were probably bruising her skin. "You left me with that man! Do you have any fucking idea what hell I have gone through? He beat me, even raped me! Every day I begged for it to stop! For you to come back!

"But you never did! I had to endear the pain every fucking day! Do you know how many scars are on my body that are caused by that man? Because of your damn mistakes, I had to pay for it!" Adrian yelled in his mother's face. White hot anger burned through him as he glared into the same eyes that used to love him. The same eyes that he had.

"I-I'm sorry." she hiccuped. "I never meant to cheat on your father. It just lead to that." Maria said in a shaky voice. A growl cut through Adrian's voice as he tightened his grip on her shoulders. "It lead to my hell," he hissed furiously. "And to his death." he added with a sneer.

Maria's eyes widened when she heard Adrian's words. "That's right," Adrian answered her unasked question. "I killed him. Stabbed him repeatedly till he was dead. And I enjoyed it." Adrian gloated. His hands ghosted up her body till they were on her throat. "I guess I should thank you, Mom. Without you, I wouldn't be who I am." Adrian said.

His hands clench down on her throat. A choked gasp escaped Maria's lips as she began to claw at his arms. "I wouldn't have met the one person I actually care about." he began to list. "And I wouldn't have been able to do this,"

His lips press against Maria's forehead as he tightened his grip on her throat. "I forgive you." he whispered before using all of his strength to break her neck.

Chapter 27

C ody

'Where are you, you damn redheaded devil,' Cody thought in annoyance but also worry. He stared out of his window in hopes of seeing the familiar red color.

A week. A damn week has passed and there has been no signs of Adrian. The police had found the ambulance he had stolen. They looked through the entire neighborhood where Adrian had ditched the truck but couldn't find anything. But they did find the dead body of a woman who had her neck snapped.

Cody has been worried sick. He kept his phone close by in case Adrian called him. And he watched the news for any reports of Adrian. Except everything they were talking about were mostly about Cody.

The news about Michael's death and what he had done spread like wildfire. A police investigation was placed in his building and the truth was discovered. He had a list of people that he made contact with to help him kill Cody's parents and get away with it. There were names of the very men who were involved with the 'robbery'. Then there were the files he made so that he could get custody of Cody, but of course so that he could try and get the money.

Cody and Michaela were interrogated the day after returning home with Sarah. Michaela stayed the night because she was too scared to be by herself while her parents were on a business trip. She had Sarah bring Marcella into the house. (Never had Cody seen an iguana and a dog get along so smoothly. The sight was just odd.)

The interrogation wasn't like the one back in Minnesota. He was victim for both crimes, except he killed a man for the second crime. Cody admitted to shooting Michael but explained it was out of defense and to protect Michaela. Michaela backed him up by telling them that Michael had put a knife to her throat.

Detective Johns and Jackson took in the information seriously. They took notes and asked questions. They didn't accuse Cody or Michaela of anything. And when Jackson asked who Adrian was, and Cody replied with,"He's the one who saved my life." After that, everything became a blur as Cody went through the week trying to forget everything that happened.

Cody doesn't turn his head when he heard his door open. "Go bother Marcella or Michaela, Izzy. I'm not in the mood." he said with a wave of his hand. The sound of giggling made him turn around and saw it wasn't Izzy. "Except I'm not Izzy. She's busy playing chase with Marcella." spoke Sarah.

"I thought you had work today?" Cody said. He saw that she was wearing sweatpants and a big t-shirt. And it was the afternoon. Sarah walks over to Cody and began to pet his head. "Took the day off. I didn't want you or Michaela to be alone."

'Don't wanna seem rude, but I hoped you weren't home in case Adrian dropped by.' Cody thought but leaned into his foster-mother's touch. "I'm fine, Sarah. And Michaela is sleeping peacefully on the sofa while watching horror movies," Cody said nonchalantly. "Most people seek out help when they went through such a scary event. But Michaela seeks horror movies to watch other people get killed and gored as a way to cope." he said with a sigh.

A not-so-pleasing look appeared on Sarah's face. "I know," she stated. "I walked passed her when the killer tore out one of the victims' eyeballs." she finished with a shudder. "Uncensored." she added. "Yeah, she's gonna need therapy." Cody said with a nod. He's been through worse than Michaela had but she had a knife to her throat. For all he knows, Michaela could be crying her eyes out.

"What about you? You don't need therapy?" Sarah asked skeptically, not believing a word Cody said. A heartless chuckle escaped Cody as he looks back out the window. "I've experienced enough trauma to know how to cope." he said sadly yet truthfully.

"SON OF A BITCH!" Michaela screams suddenly.

Sarah and Cody were momentarily startled before quickly running out of the room. They practically flew down the stairs with Cody in the lead. Cody jumped down the last four steps and had a rough landing. He shakes it off, stands up, and runs into the living room. And nearly trips again at what he finds.

There was no danger. Instead Michaela was hugging a tall person with long blond hair. He was a foot taller than Michaela and had broad shoulders. Dressed clad in black, the man almost looked like death.

"Do you have any idea how worried we've been?" Michaela said in relief. She shakes the man's shoulders before making eye contact with Cody. Her face was soaked in tears but she had a bright smile on her face. "Michaela, who is that?" asked Sarah, yet Cody had a feeling who it is. He steps up to the man and grabs his shoulder. "Adrian?" Cody whispered as the person turns around. Those familiar ice blue eyes met Cody's brown ones.

Relief flashes across Cody's face as he practically jumped on Adrian. His arms wrapped tightly around Adrian's neck and he kissed him roughly yet passionately. Adrian didn't waste a second on responding to the kiss.

"Since when did you have a boyfriend?" Sarah spoke up in surprise. "Oh, they're not dating. At least, I think they're not." Michaela said in amusement and confusion. The need for air broke Cody's concentration and he breaks away from the kiss. He ignores Sarah and Michaela, and kept his eyes on Adrian. "You had me worried sick. And what's with the blond hair?" Cody asked in a hushed voice.

Running his fingers through his newly blond locks, Adrian smiled brightly. "Had to ditch the red hair. It was becoming an eyesore anyway," he admitted with a shrug. He places his fingers on Cody's neck and lightly traces the bruises. They were faint but still hurt if pressure was applied. "Glad to see you're alright." Adrian said happily.

"Okay! Okay! Can someone tell me what is going on? Who is this guy?!" Sarah demanded almost exasperated. She was actually waving her arms around like a crazy person. 'She's getting hysterical. As long as she doesn't know exactly who Adrian is, everything should be fine,' Cody thought as he turned around to face his mother. "Sarah, this is Adrian, my boyfriend." Cody said.

Epilogue

Two months have passed since the whole Michael-incident. Cody and Michaela returned to school, and instantly became the most interesting people there. No one treated them like before, the bullies backed off–even Jack. The boy had returned after five weeks and was a new person. He stopped being a jerk to everyone. Especially to Cody because he saved Jack's life.

Cody officially turned eighteen four weeks ago and claimed his birthright. One million dollars was deposited into his account and everything was right with the world.

The murder case of Takanawa ended with Keiko being processed twenty to life in prison. Adrian was careful in staying under the police's radar. He escaped from conviction once again. Making Takanawa his thirtieth kill.

Days went back to being boring and casual as they usually were before. . .

Cody was so close to falling asleep when he felt two arms wrap around his waist. Cody opens his eyes as he was pulled into someone's chest. Soon, a tick grew on his face as he turns around and shoves Adrian off of him.

"Just because Sarah said you could stay the night does not mean you can sleep in my bed!" Cody yelled as he pushes a sleeping Adrian out of his bed. The familiar thump of his body hitting the floor and Adrian groaning made Cody laugh despite the drowsiness. Despite being a killer, Adrian can be amusing. Cody still didn't understand why Adrian had such an interest in him, but he no longer complains when Adrian saved his life.

Two large hands popped up and began to claw the bed. Slowly, Adrian pulls himself back up with a grunt. His blond hair was shorter but his bangs hung over his eyes. There were a few less tattoos on his torso and arms. Cody wouldn't have recognized him if he hadn't seen Adrian naked before.

"Can't a man sleep next to his lovely boyfriend?" Adrian asked. He crawls back in bed and lays himself on top of Cody. His relaxing state ended when Cody dug his nails into his windpipe. "Not unless his 'lovely boyfriend' allows it." Cody growled as he pulls Adrian off of his lap. "Ow! Ow! Ow! Ow!" Adrian repeated with a hiss. When Cody finally lets go, Adrian gasped and falls down beside his boyfriend. "Where did you learn that move?" Adrian asked as he rubbed the red mark on his neck. "Michaela taught me. She took up on self-defense classes." Cody said. He turns his body to face Adrian and smirks. "Now I can kick your ass for being sly." he said evilly.

A smirk slowly grew on Adrian's face, which causes Cody's confidence to slowly shrivel. Before Cody knew it, he was sitting up on Adrian's lap with hands squeezing his hips. "Son of a bitch!" he gasped. "Language." Adrian said before pulling Cody in for a kiss. His hands held Cody's head so their kiss could be longer. Cody's breath was taken away as he settled into the kiss.

Their tongues met after a furious make-out and began to wrestle each other. Grunts and moans escaped them both as they began to grind their bodies together. Cody trails his fingers down Adrian's chest till he reached the waistband of his boxers. He stops their tongue-twisting and locks eyes with Adrian. The two both had lust raging in their eyes that couldn't be ignored.

"Can I?" Adrian asked as he fingers Cody's waistband. "Yes." Cody said before pushing down Adrian's underwear.

Cody's face caught fire when they were both completely naked. And I thought murder felt so extreme, Cody thought nervously. He reaches down to cover his privates, but Adrian grabbed his hands before Cody could. "Don't cover yourself. You're beautiful," Adrian complimented. "Says the killer who could've seen many other bodies." Cody mumbled. He barely catches a glimpse of Adrian's frown before he's being rolled onto his back with Adrian on top.

Landing on his back with widen eyes, Cody stares at Adrian breathlessly. "Id have you know that I have only seen my victims naked. I've never been as intimate with anyone as I am with you." Adrian said. "Don't kill the mood by talking about your victims." Cody snapped before wrapping his legs around Adrian's waist and tossing them both over the bed.

The two rolled off of the bed and landed with Adrian below them. "Holy shit." Adrian breathed. "That's more like it." Cody laughed before he began to bite down on Adrian's neck. "aaaHHHH!" yelped Adrian, not able to hold in his cries.

'Who's the screamer now,' Cody thought amusingly as he bends down and began run his tongue down Adrian's stomach to his thighs.

Despite his throbbing heart, Cody felt him slowly begin to panic. His first time is with a killer. Never going back now. He takes in a deep breath and takes Adrian into his mouth. "Shit!" Adrian hissed as he felt his cock being swallowed. It was his turn to wrap his legs around Cody's waist, except he began to dig his heels into Cody's lower back. "Faster!" Adrian ordered.

'I swear if you start kicking me like a horse. I'll bite off this damn thing.' Cody thought as he began to bob his head up and down on his lover's cock.

The room soon became filled with Adrian's lust-filled moans. Cody could hear him claw the floor and was mentally cursing as Adrian was digging his heels deeper into his back. 'That's it!' he growled before breaking away with a pop. Adrian stops his moans and looked at Cody in confusion. His face was bright red and covered in sweat. "Why did you stop?" he asked. "For this," Cody began before flipping Adrian onto his stomach."I'm gonna fuck you like an animal." Cody finished.

"Then don't hold back." Adrian said happily.

With a roar, Cody entered Adrian full force. Their hips met with a heavy 'slap'. Adrian cried out as both pain and pleasure shot through his body. "Fuck!" he yelled. "Want me to go slow?" Cody asked amusingly. "Hell no! Go fast! I don't care if I brake!" Adrian encourages as he pulls back to continue hitting Cody's hips.

Cody thrusted into Adrian in a fast and continuous pace. He bends forward and bites down on Adrian's shoulder as he quickens his pace. The taste of salty and hot flesh on his tongue thrilled Cody to an extent. A growl rumbled through his throat as he bit down harder.

"HaaaaaaAAAAAAA!" Adrian cried as he ejaculated. His body went rigid, and he arches his back as shockwaves of pleasure shot through him. Cody held firm and made sure that Adrian didn't move. "Don't move." he ordered huskily in Adrian's ear. His tongue licked the shell of Adrian's ear and nibbles his earlobe.

Their hands linked together as Cody continued thrusting. Cody's face buried into the crook of Adrian's neck, inhaling his scent. He runs his tongue over the jugular vein, feeling the flow of blood pulse from under the skin. "Not only do you taste delicious, you sound amazing." Cody whispered in Adrian's ear as his lover kept gasping in ecstasy.

Suddenly, Cody pulls away and flips Adrian on to his back. Surprise was on Adrian's flushed face as he stared questionably at Cody. "What are you doing?" he asked confused. "Didn't you want me to ride you?" Cody asked curiously. He crawls on top of Adrian's chest with his hands groping Adrian's cock. "You talk in your sleep." Cody suddenly stated when he saw Adrian's startled face.

"Where has this side of yours been? I love it!" Adrian said excitedly. He grabs Cody's hips and rubs his cock against Cody's aching hole. "Now it's my turn to hear you scream." he said before he pushes Cody down on his awaiting hard-on.

"AaaaaHHHHHH!" Cody yelled as he was filled up. It was a tight fit but was a pleasant fill. "My turn to move." Adrian said huskily before he began to thrust inside of Cody. "Faster! Faster!" Cody urged as he dug his nails into Adrian's chest. "My pleasure." Adrian said gleefully.

It felt like his body was about to explode in nothing but pleasure. He bends forward and kisses Adrian deeply. Their tongues swirled around each other's mouths as Adrian continued thrusting into Cody. "I love you, Adrian." Cody said suddenly when they break away from air. Adrian stops mid-thrust and stares at Cody in surprise.

"I love you." Cody repeated with a smile. A smile slowly grew on Adrian's face. He slowly sits up and hugs Cody tightly. "I love you too." Adrian said happily.

The two men shared another kiss before settling on the floor. Slowly falling asleep with the silence . . .

"Can we go find someone to kill later?" Adrian asked hopefully.

"As long as the person is an asshole and is doing something bad then fine." Cody replied gruffly. "Now shut up and go to bed." he snapped.

www.ingramcontent.com/pod-product-compliance
Lightning Source LLC
Chambersburg PA
CBHW071016180726
48291CB00004B/1482